OUTRIDERS
EXPEDITION TO PINE HOLLOW

ED DECTER

ILLUSTRATED BY SAMMY YUEN JR.

ALADDIN PAPERBACKS
New York London Toronto Sydney

ALADDIN PAPERBACKS
An imprint of Simon & Schuster Children's Publishing Division
1230 Avenue of the Americas, New York, NY 10020
Text copyright © 2007 by Frontier Pictures, Inc. and Ed Decter
Illustrations copyright © 2007 by Simon & Schuster, Inc.
All rights reserved, including the right of reproduction in whole or in part in any form.
ALADDIN PAPERBACKS and related logo are registered trademarks of Simon & Schuster, Inc.
Outriders is a trademark of Ed Decter.
Designed by Sammy Yuen Jr.
The text of this book was set in Janson Text.
Manufactured in the United States of America
First Aladdin Paperbacks edition August 2007
10 9 8 7 6 5 4 3 2 1
Library of Congress Control Number 2007924702
ISBN-13: 978-1-4169-1307-8
ISBN-10: 1-4169-1307-6

*For Jackie and June, sisters, friends,
and original Outriders*

Very special thanks to:

Hanay Geiogamah, Professor of Theater, UCLA Department of American Indian Studies, for pointing me to all the right research materials.

John J. Strauss, for all things surfing (and for being the best screenwriting partner and friend, ever).

Ervin Rustemagic, for all things Slovenian, an inspiration to artists and writers all throughout the world.

Paul Tyler, for letting me sit at John O'Groats and write for hours, and for naming a dish on the menu after me.

Frank Beddor, author, *The Looking Glass Wars*, for starting me on this whole expedition and showing me how it is *really* done.

Jerry Tarnoff, Superintendent of Schools, West Orange, NJ, for making my hometown a great place to be a kid and go on expeditions.

Jen Klonsky, best editor on earth, who can make even the hard deadlines fun.

Barbara Marshall, best agent on the planet, who always listens, even when I don't.

Cheryl Doherty and Abby Decter, who deserve thanks each and every moment.

THE OUTRIDERS BLOG

BOARD NOT BORED

EXPEDITION: PINE HOLLOW

Entry by: Cam Walker

Note: If you have been surfing the web and come across this blog and happen to be affiliated with the following agencies: U.S. State Department, U.S. Department of the Interior, Bureau of Land Management, Office of the Attorney General, Department of Health and Human Services, Bureau of Indian Affairs, Federal Aviation Administration, or the U.S. Coast Guard, please keep in mind that the author of this post is only twelve and may be making it all up.

Ellistown

Ellistown Airport

*Surf Island
Lagoon*

Goats Neck

Bluffs Yacht
Club

Cedar Cape

*Goats Neck
Bridge*

The Bluffs

Surf Island

Santuary Cove

Rocky Point
Beach

*Cedar Cape
Coast Guard Station*

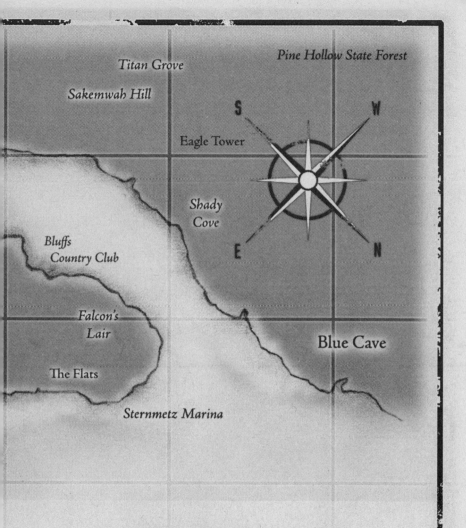

MAP OF SURF ISLAND

CHAPTER ONE: GALLOPING

I didn't know which came first—the spotlights or the alarm siren. What I did know was that the security guards at the Bluffs Country Club were going to find us in about thirty seconds. I could hear the whine of their electric golf carts zooming toward our location. Walkie-talkies crackled to life. I heard a security guard yell, "They're near the sixteenth fairway!"

Even though it was eleven o'clock at night, the woods surrounding the golf course (golfer dudes called it the rough) were lit up like it was high noon. I could see hundreds of white golf balls glinting in the glare of the high-powered security lights. Each golf ball was worth twenty-five cents to our friend Chuck at Surf Island Discount Golf and Tennis. It was like a cruel joke that I wouldn't have time to pick up even one of them. It is hard to farm golf balls when you are being chased by the entire security force of a country club.

In theory, my plan should have worked. After dark the golf course is completely deserted. Wyatt, Bettina, and I had done some advanced intel and determined that the night security guards only patrolled the area near the clubhouse. All we had to do was slip under a new "guest entrance" we had dug beneath the perimeter chain-link fence, click on some flashlights, and load our backpacks full of slightly used golf balls. But I had made one serious miscalculation: I had ignored history.

My friends and I have had some close calls at the Bluffs Country Club. Recently we had almost been caught after hauling out about a thousand golf balls from the water hazard fronting the seventh green. That brush with danger had led to the discovery of our zip line that connected a secret ledge up in the Bluffs to the Good Climbing Tree in my best friend Shelby's backyard down in the Flats. The zip line, which was actually an old steel winch cable that we had scavenged from Wyatt's dad's marine salvage yard, was now coiled in a rusty pile near a patch of wild strawberries two hundred feet below our current position. The country club security force had actually used a *blowtorch* to slice through the winch cable. I should have remembered this crucial detail while I was formulating my night ball-farming plan. There were much easier ways to detach the zip line. A simple socket wrench would have done it. The use of the blow torch indicated a certain level of anger and commitment to protecting the sanctity of the Bluffs Club. So I shouldn't have been so shocked that the club had installed an infrared beam, security spotlights, and a siren alarm that sounded as if seven hundred tomcats decided to have a fight all at the same time.

Wyatt was lucky. His backpack had gotten snagged on a branch at the top of the Escape Trail. While he was getting untangled, Bettina and I had slipped under the fence and made our way to the edge of the sixteenth fairway, where, just behind a sand trap, there was a patch of high grass that always yielded a treasure trove of golf balls. Bettina and I had just unzipped our backpacks to start harvesting when we tripped the beam and triggered the alarm. We were about forty yards from the chain-link fence and Wyatt. There was no way for our friend to rescue us, and there was no point in the three of us getting caught trespassing. So I was confident that Wyatt would recognize the danger, slip back into the shadows, and make his way down the Escape Trail. Bettina and I would not have that option. We could see two golf carts OUTSIDE the perimeter fence, converging on the newly dug guest entrance. There were about five more golf carts zipping across the fairway directly toward us. As I saw it, here were our options:

Option 1: Run
Option 2: See Option 1

I didn't want to make any loud noises that would attract the attention of the security guards, so I just pointed in the direction of the sixteenth green. Bettina nodded. I had chosen Bettina for this mission because she can move around more quickly and more quietly than anyone else in the Outriders. Shelby claims it is because Bettina is *graceful*, but I think if Bettina heard anyone but Shelby say that, she would punch them in the arm. No amount of silence or gracefulness was going to get us out of our current problem. A flashlight beam hit us; we had been spotted. Five golf carts were now vectoring in our direction.

Bettina and I started SPRINTING. I'm not bragging or anything, but I'm a pretty fast runner. Surfing builds a lot of strength in your legs, so I can truly motor if called upon. The thing is, Bettina is *wicked* fast. She's like some kind of freakish gazelle, and I had a lot of trouble keeping up with her. I didn't have any time to let this bother me; we were about five seconds away from being overrun by the security guards in their golf carts.

"Jenkins! Purcell! Fan out!" I heard one of them yell.

Two golf carts split from the armada and moved to our flanks. In a matter of seconds we would be encircled by angry security guards.

"Grab them! NOW!" Out of the corner of my eye I spotted either Jenkins or Purcell jumping out of his golf cart and dashing toward Bettina and me.

Sometimes kids make the mistake of underestimating the intelligence of adults, but *almost always* adults make the mistake of underestimating the intelligence of kids. Here's what the security guards who were chasing us *assumed*: We were two kids from down in the Flats who didn't know our way around up in the Bluffs. But they were dead wrong. Bettina and I weren't just running *away*— we actually *knew where we were headed*.

UNSCHEDULED RETURN TO FALCON'S LAIR

It just so happened we were personal acquaintances of the absolute-no-doubt-about-it wealthiest, most powerful person who lived in the Bluffs, Mr. Chapman Thorpe. His ginormous estate—which didn't even have a street address, just a name: Falcon's Lair—was situated right alongside the golf course, just behind the sixteenth green on the other side of the low stone wall we were running toward.

The great thing about best friends is they know what you are thinking without you ever having to say a word. Bettina just *knew* we were going to vault over the wall. Without breaking stride, she planted her hands on the top of it and slipped over like some kind of Olympic gymnast. Not wanting to be out-done, I went for the same smooth move, but since I'm a guy, I'm not as limber; one of my legs didn't quite clear the top. I felt my ankle scrape the rough stones and knew I had left behind a nice hunk of skin.

The guy who was on foot (Jenkins or Purcell) must have been too heavy or too out of shape to make the vault. I figured this out when I heard him scream something like "OOOOORF" when he made it to the wall. Then I heard him shout, "I'm down!"

Our bold maneuver had bought us a little time. The sprawling grounds behind Mr. Thorpe's estate were not illuminated by the security spotlights, so Bettina and I were now in total darkness. We had visited Falcon's Lair before (once on a school trip in fourth grade, and a few times when we had dealings with Mr. Thorpe), so we knew the basic layout of the fifty-acre estate. Now I don't want you to get the wrong idea. Bettina and I weren't "friends" with Mr. Thorpe. We weren't even sure we trusted him. He had helped the Outriders out on an expedition and we had helped him uncover some clues that might lead to a hidden treasure (more about that stuff later), but it's not like Bettina and I could run up to his back door and seek asylum. But what we could do was find a place to hide until the security guards gave up their search.

I could hear the guards' tensed-out voices from the golf course behind us.

"Get Purcell a medic!"

"There is no *medic*, sir!"

"Call base and have them alert Falcon's Lair!"

"There's no one at base, sir. We're all here!"

"Just give me a flashlight, you idiot!"

I glanced over my shoulder and could see six flashlight beams click on in unison. The security guards had no intention of giving up.

Bettina tapped me on the shoulder and pointed toward a long, low structure far to our right. We cut toward it. I remembered that Mr. Thorpe had hundreds of hidden security cameras all over his property. I wondered if they had night-vision capability. Were Mr. Thorpe and his butler dude, Giorgio, watching us from the office in his solarium? Were they going to call the police? It was too big and frightening a thought, so I pushed it aside as Bettina and I reached the dark building. I couldn't see very well, but I could *smell* that we had reached a stable.

As soon as we slipped inside the huge sliding wooden barn doors and closed them behind us, I felt as if I was being watched. I looked down the row of the darkened stables. Thin slivers of lavender moonlight poked through the rafters and illuminated a row of glowing caramel-colored eyes. All those eyes were staring right at Bettina and me. I could make out the silhouettes of about twenty horses' heads poking out of their wooden stalls. A few of the horses began to snort. My guess is that the horses were alert or nervous or maybe hungry. I don't know much about horses.

GALLOWAY

I felt Bettina grab my T-shirt and pull me toward one of the stalls. A wooden sign hung on the front of the stall. The word "Galloway" was burnished into the wood. My guess was that this was the name of the horse inside the stall. As we approached, I could see that the horse had a kind of reddish-brown color with a dark mane and tail. I should also mention that Galloway was ULTRA-HUGE. I'm not short like Wyatt, but I would have had to *jump full-out* to pat this horse on the top of the head. Galloway looked like he weighed more than a bulldozer and his hooves seemed like they could have used pie plates for horseshoes. I also notice that the horse's ears were pinned back, and even though I don't know much about horses, I have seen that same look on a dog and I knew it wasn't good.

"Shhhh," Bettina whispered.

"I didn't say a word," I whispered back.

But Bettina hadn't been talking to me. She had moved to one side of the giant horse's head and extended her hand just beneath the horse's nostrils. It looked as if she were letting the horse smell her, much like someone would do with a dog.

I knew the search party would eventually come to look here in the stables, so we didn't have much time to stop and socialize with the farm animals.

"Bettina, I—"

"Shhh!" This time Bettina had been silencing me. She began gently stroking the horse's muzzle (do horses have muzzles? I have no idea), and I watched the gargantuan animal's ears rise up. The beast seemed to relax. In fact the gigantic horse actually lowered his head and swung it closer to Bettina, obviously enjoying her touch. Bettina pressed her cheek against Galloway's cheek (do horse's have cheeks?) and they remained like that for a moment. Bettina has long, dark curly hair (Shelby calls her an African-American Aphrodite, whatever that means), and Galloway seemed to enjoy nuzzling his head in her curls. Even though we were in severe danger of being discovered, the sight of a ninety-pound girl being able to control this equine bulldozer was so impressive, I had to watch for a moment in silent awe. Then Bettina did the last thing on earth I would have EVER done—she opened the door to Galloway's stall and pulled me inside.

I promise I'm not bragging, but I'm a pretty brave guy. I'll charge into a big swell when all the other surfers at Rocky Point Beach take a pass. I sort of understand the ocean. I respect its power, but I feel like I have a handle on what it might do. I did not feel that way about Galloway. I certainly respected his power, but I had no clue what he was thinking or what he might do. That's why I was so afraid—the kind of afraid where you forget to breath or swallow.

Bettina couldn't have been calmer or more relaxed. She closed the stall door behind us with one hand while keeping the other on Galloway's muscular shoulder (if that is what it is called). The colossal animal now swung his head to the rear, keeping one huge eye on us (mostly me) at all times. I realized I had a tense smile frozen on my face. I guess deep down my survival instinct had triggered my brain to send out a command to my facial muscles in a pathetic attempt to do *something* to try and make Galloway *like* and *trust* me. I knew dogs could smell fear and a horse has a much bigger nose than a dog, so I was pretty certain Galloway knew exactly how I felt. As if to show me, he shifted his weight slightly. This caused his rump to brush against the side of my body and sent me sprawling backward, slamming me into the wooden side of the stall.

"Don't make any sudden moves," Bettina whispered.

"Tell *him* that," I whispered back as I made an internal inventory of bones and organs.

"Irish warmblood."

I had no idea what Bettina was talking about.

She sighed and said, "The breed. He's a hunter."

"I didn't know horses ate meat," I said.

Bettina closed her eyes. I was disappointing her in some way. I just didn't know how.

"Galloway's trained as a hunter. That's his *event*," Bettina whispered as she stroked his mane.

You might wonder how someone from the Flats like Bettina knew so much about horses. People who live in our neighborhood are not known for being "equestrians" or "horse people." In fact Bettina is the only one of us who has ever ridden a horse (unless you count being strapped on top of a pony at the county fair). Bettina's uncle worked at a horse ranch near Cedar Cape. Bettina spent most of her summers living and working out there. When we were in art class, Bettina *drew* horses. When we had a creative writing assignment in English class, Bettina *wrote* about horses. Sure, Bettina *enjoyed* archery, but she *loved* horses. This is why Galloway rump-bumped *me* and not Bettina. The horse was clearly the smartest one in the stall.

"See the chestnut coat, the dark mane? He's a bay. Isn't he magnificent?"

Before I could answer Bettina, I heard voices outside the stables. The security guards had reached the building. Through the slatted wood of the stable walls I could see flickers of their flashlights.

Without saying a word, Bettina ran one hand along the side of the horse and with the other pulled me toward the back of the stall. I understood what she was trying to do. She was attempting to hide us behind the giant Irish warmblood. It was a good plan because we were completely concealed in Galloway's vast shadow. Unless the security guards had some type of death wish and intended to open and inspect every stall (which didn't seem likely), there would be a chance that we could escape detection.

We heard the large wooden barn doors slide open at the far end of the stables. I could see circles of flashlight beams dancing across the stalls. Galloway and the other horses began snorting and shifting their weight. I plastered myself against the back of the stall, just praying that I would not be pulverized into oblivion by the largest horse ever to roam the earth. Bettina kept stroking Galloway, trying to keep him calm, and not wanting him to angle in a direction that would reveal us.

"Look in each and every one of those stalls!" The leader of the security guards yelled.

A bunch of the horses started to whinny.

"Roger that, Roger," one of the guards replied with a snicker.

"That was funny *once*, Jenkins!" screamed the leader who apparently was named Roger.

Disturbed by all the noise, the horses started to whinny even louder.

"Shut up, you dumb animals!" Roger yelled.

I couldn't see very much in the darkened stall, but I *knew* Bettina had narrowed her eyes and set her jaw at that last comment.

I could see one of the flashlight beams getting closer to our stall.

"You know cows is smarter than horses?" Roger said to the guards. "Pigs, too. Fact is, horses is the dumbest critters on the farm."

Now the beam of light lit up the inside of Galloway's stall. Bettina and I were careful to stay behind the equine's massive flank (or side, I'm not sure what you call it). The only thing I knew about horses was not to get directly behind them because they could kick, and this was confirmed by Bettina's body position: She was careful to stand just to the side of Galloway's powerful rear legs. We hadn't yet been spotted, but we were now relying on *luck*, which is the hallmark of any truly bad plan.

"See, Jenkins? Look at these big, dumb eyes," Roger said as he pointed the flashlight directly into Galloway's face. Even I knew this was a HUGE mistake. With the speed of a lightning bolt, Galloway KICKED the stall door in front of him, and it sounded as if someone had shot off a BAZOOKA inside the stables. There was a seven-inch HOLE in the door where the hoof had made contact.

Roger jumped back about five feet. I could hear him taking big inhales of air. Galloway's head was raised, his ears back. I could feel Bettina's body tense. We couldn't have been in a more dangerous spot if we'd been in a swimming pool with an orca.

"Oh, you think you're some kind of tough guy?" Roger said.

I could see the other flashlight beams converging outside the stall door. Three strangers were standing in front of Galloway and he did not like it one bit. I felt the horse's muscles tense like a bunch of titanium springs. Bettina kept trying to calm the horse with her touch. It was not working. Galloway was snorting and sort of spitting at the same time. His front hoof pawed at the straw at the bottom of the stall.

Then Roger made an even HUGER mistake, perhaps the HUGEST mistake he would ever make, one that I am positive he will remember and regret for the rest of his life. Roger flicked his flashlight and *smacked Galloway on the nose*.

What I am about to tell you all took place in about ten seconds. Bettina shoved me back against the wall just as Galloway reared up on his hind legs. This made him a twelve-foot-tall volcano of pure fury. Galloway shot his front legs forward. The stall door popped off its hinges as easily as if it were made of paper. The wooden door slammed into the three security guards and instantly bowled them over. The three of them were now flat on the ground, the wooden door lying on top of them. As I've made clear, I know nothing about the psychology of horses, but even I was sure what Galloway was going to do next. He wanted to TRAMPLE the security guards. I sensed some movement to my left and I saw Bettina toss some sort of thick blanket on Galloway's back. This unexpected sensation seemed to stop the horse in its tracks. I didn't know it at the moment, but Bettina had just saved the three guards' lives.

Galloway looked around quizzically in our direction. For an instant I thought he would focus his rage on us. Then Bettina did yet another thing it would never occur to me to do: She put one leg on a metal hay rack, pushed herself onto the horse's back, and swung her legs onto either side of the humungous animal. For some reason Galloway was so confused by this that his rage dissipated. He started to fidget, unaccustomed to this new rider on his back. I was trapped at the side of the stall—there was no way I could get safely around the leviathan.

I now heard the voices of a bunch of other security guards rushing into the stables. Walkie-talkie's crackled.

"MEN DOWN! MEN DOWN!"

"MEDIC! MEDIC!"

"We don't have a medic!"

Bettina reached down and grabbed my hand. It seemed she had the ridiculous idea for me to join her atop of the world's biggest and scariest horse. I would have resisted this insane idea if I had any other choice for escape, but I was confined in a horse's stall with about eight security guards waiting just outside to take me into custody. It was a pick-your-poison type of moment, so I planted my foot on the metal hay rack, sort of belly flopped onto the back of the horse, and trusted that my friend Bettina could somehow ride a two-thousand-pound bull-dozer disguised as a horse without saddle, stirrups, or reins. I'm not afraid to admit I had sweat through my underwear. At least I hoped it was sweat.

The most exciting moment when you are out on a surfboard is when you drop into a wave. The nose of your board breaks the crest of the wave and then all of a sudden there is a wall of water rising behind you as you stand up on the board. Then you drop in, and this huge surge of power takes you across the face of the wave. Even if you are a pro surfer you realize you are on the edge of something dangerous and powerful. You don't control the wave—it controls you. Riding on top of Galloway was like what I imagined it would be like to drop in at the Banzai Pipeline on the North Shore of Oahu—there was a better than average chance it would be the last day of your life.

Galloway BOLTED out of the stall. Somehow, someway, Bettina was holding on to his black mane and steered the massive horse AWAY from the fallen stall door. While Bettina had a grip on the horse, the only thing I could think to hold on to was Bettina. I circled my arms around her waist in some kind of death grip. I was worried that I was going to squeeze all the air out of her body, but I had lost conscious control of my muscles by this point—I was acting on pure unadulterated FEAR. The other security guards had the good sense to DIVE out of the way as Galloway charged toward the open stable door.

Within three strides Galloway had burst out of the stable and was running at full speed. The confrontation with Roger had so agitated the horse that he was galloping with a kind of wild intensity, sometimes bucking his back legs in the air as if wanting to toss off the two mosquitoes on his back.

Amazingly Bettina managed to keep a calm tone to her voice as she spoke to Galloway.

"It's okay, handsome boy. It's okay. Time for a nice ride now."

I was convinced that Bettina's gentle words would not penetrate the angry mood of the horse, but somehow Galloway sort of smoothed out his gait. He was still charging forward like a runaway train, but at least the locomotive wasn't trying to throw us off like before. There was about a four-second period where I almost enjoyed myself on top of the powerful animal. And then I saw the wall.

Remember the *low* wall that Bettina and I had vaulted behind the sixteenth green? This wasn't the same wall. *This* stone wall was a *much taller wall*. It was the one that bordered Pine Barren Lane, the main road that meandered around the Bluffs. This wall was SIX FEET HIGH, and for some freaky reason, Galloway was RUNNING RIGHT TOWARD IT!

"TURN HIM!" I said. I think I was screaming.

"I'M TRYING!" Bettina said. There was absolutely fear in her voice.

I once saw this documentary on TV about the Abrams M1A1 battle tank. It is the main battle tank of the U.S. Army. It's really big and powerful. But the thing I remembered most was that they showed the Abrams M1A1 battle tank crashing through the sides of buildings. I guess I flashed on this memory because it appeared that Galloway had every intention of trying to RAM his way through the solid stone wall.

"HOLD ON!" Bettina yelled.

"IS THERE ANOTHER CHOICE?" I yelled back.

Then the scariest thing of all happened. Galloway's head went DOWN. Bettina slid forward and the only way she could hold on was to try to circle her arms around the powerful neck of the horse. I slid forward as well, and for an instant I thought I was going to flip heels over head and fly OVER Bettina, but somehow I managed to reach underneath her and grab a hank of the horse's mane. At that very instant Galloway's head came UP. I felt a surge of explosive power underneath me and that's when we left the ground.

It wasn't even close. Galloway cleared the six-foot wall with about a foot to spare. Whatever a "hunter" horse does must include jumping, because Galloway was insanely good at it. I wish I could describe to you all of the visual sensations of flying over a stone wall and landing cleanly on the grass on the other side, but I had my eyes closed the entire time.

Bettina and I should have been able to breathe a huge sigh of relief. We had gotten away from the Bluffs Country Club security guards, no one had been seriously hurt, and it appeared as if we would be able to escape to the Flats without being caught, but Galloway had other plans.

At least the massive Irish warmblood seemed to be in a better mood. His head was high; his ears were up as we galloped down Pine Barren Lane.

"Can you stop him?" I said.

Bettina didn't bother answering me as it was perhaps the stupidest question I had ever asked. Galloway would stop whenever he felt like stopping. Our job was not to fall off. It was a long way down.

Now that were weren't heading on a collision course for any six-foot walls, I have to admit that riding atop Galloway was the only thing I've ever done that matched the rush of surfing. I could understand why Bettina was so obsessed with horses—they live in a land beyond cool.

If anyone in the Bluffs was awake and looking out the windows of their estates, they would have seen a very odd sight: two twelve-year-olds riding bare-back on top of an ultra-huge horse galloping down the center of Pine Barren Lane. It might have also seemed odd to watch the horse come to a complete stop at the intersection of Mid-Valley Road and permit the two riders to dismount. But the oddest thing of all would have been to watch the now rider-less horse turn around and casually trot off toward Falcon's Lair as if it had made these wild midnight rides many times.

For some freaky reason, as if he knew where we were headed, Galloway had deposited us right at the road that snaked from the Bluffs down into the Flats. Even though it was a warm night, I was so drenched with sweat I found myself shivering. Also one of my socks was turning red from the scrape on my ankle. Well, not the scrape, but the blood.

"Wow," was all I could think to say.

"You have no idea how lucky we were," Bettina said.

"I think I kind of do."

"We sort of failed at the mission, though."

"Big time," I said, and we started the long march down from the Bluffs.

Right about now, you might be wondering why we

needed golf balls so badly that we would risk entering a private country club at night, getting chased by a phalanx of security guards, and taking a wild ride on the world's largest horse. Expeditions need supplies and supplies cost money. The expedition we had planned was to the absolute, no-doubt-about-it, most important place to all of us. It was the place where the Outriders had become the Outriders. Deep inside of Pine Hollow State Forest there is a hill called Sakemwah Hill and on top of it there is a mysterious structure called Eagle Tower. The thing is, we absolutely *had to* get the gear we needed and go on this expedition because we knew Eagle Tower was going to be *torn down* five days from now. What we didn't know is that we would discover a lost city and almost be trapped in there for eternity. But I'll get to that stuff later.

CHAPTER TWO: FREEZING

I was the first to arrive at Island Freeze. The Freeze is the official meeting place of the Outriders. We were all supposed to meet to discuss a new strategy for raising money now that the night farming mission was a bust.

"'Sup," my brother, Kyle, said. He's the assistant manager at the Freeze.

"Not much," I said.

Kyle had been gathering up all the napkin containers so he could refill them. He had to abandon the task as two customers came to the food service window. As Kyle drifted over to take their order, I slumped down on a bench. I was sort of glad Kyle was busy; I wasn't in the mood for any kind of conversation. I wanted to be alone in my failure.

I know that sounds extra harsh, but the truth is, the rest of the Outriders sort of expect me to be the one who makes the plans. I'm not one of those guys who can figure out how to design a vacuum cleaner that still has 100 percent suction even when full of dirt, but when it comes to figuring out how to plan out and finance an expedition, I'm the go-to guy. But the night farming mission had failed (miserably) and we were no closer to getting the rock-climbing gear needed to explore Eagle Tower for the last time.

Sometimes if we need something for an expedition we scavenge it. The problem with rock-climbing gear is that it gets thrashed while you are out in the field. A lot of times you even have to abandon anchors or carabiners (the clips you attach to rope). If we scavenged some gear and didn't return it in really good condition, that would be stealing, which was not an option (we Outriders have a code of honor), so we had to BUY our rock-climbing equipment, but we couldn't because the one guy everyone counted on to make the plans (me) had so totally failed up in the Bluffs. You might be wondering why I was being ultra-rough on myself. It's because going to Eagle Tower was so crucial.

WHY EAGLE TOWER MATTERED SO MUCH

Sakemwah Hill is the tallest point in Pine Hollow State Forest. I'm pretty sure that the hill got its name from the Sakemwah Indians, who were the first people to live in the area around my hometown of Surf Island. Not a whole lot is known about the Sakemwah. Ms. Renape, our history teacher at Surf Island Middle School, told us that early explorers wrote about encounters with the Sakemwah and then the whole tribe just seemed to have disappeared.

From the Pine Hollow ranger station it is a four-hour hike to the top of Sakemwah Hill. At the very top of the hill you find Eagle Tower. The tower is about sixteen feet square at the base and rises to about forty feet. If you picture four sugar cubes stacked on top of one another, that's exactly the shape of the structure. There are three huge mysteries that have never been solved about the tower:

1. No one knows who built it. Was it the Sakem-wah Tribe? Was it the early explorers? Was it some long-ago soldiers?
2. The tower is constructed of a light-colored stone that can't be found anywhere on Sakem-wah Hill or in all of Pine Hollow State Forest. Where did the stone come from?
3. There is only one entrance into the tower. It is a narrow opening *thirty-five feet above the ground*. The only way to get inside is with a huge ladder or with rock-climbing gear (the way we Outriders preferred). Why was the entrance so high? What was that about?

Oh, I forgot. There is another strange thing about the tower. No one knows how it got its name. There are a whole lot of species of birds in Pine Hollow State Forest (I don't know much about birds) but no one has ever seen an eagle. Why was it called Eagle Tower?

Sometimes people or places are cool because of what you KNOW about them. I've never been to Washington, D.C., but I would guess if you go visit the Lincoln Memorial, there would be a brochure or plaque that tells you stuff like who carved the statue of the sixteenth president and what date it was built.

But Eagle Tower was awesome because of what we DIDN'T KNOW. The mystery is what made it so cool.

A few years back Wyatt, who is an encyclopedia of facts and figures about the Sakemwah (he even knows more than Ms. Renape), was telling Shelby (my best friend, remember?) and me about all the missing pieces of information regarding the long-lost Indian tribe. Missing information bothers Wyatt. It bothers him a lot. He needs to know how everything fits together. In his mind the world is just one big catalog of data. Unsolved questions, like "What happened to a whole Indian civilization?", are like pages that have been ripped out of the catalog. These pages have to be recovered and glued back or Wyatt cannot relax.

Wyatt had made Shelby and me so curious about the mystery surrounding the tower that we planned our first hike into Pine Hollow State Forest. Now remember, we were only in fourth or fifth grade at the time. So we thought it would be better if we brought along a big group of our best friends. We invited our buddies Din and Nar (it's okay if you call them the Bonglukiet twins), their 243-pound dog (a mastiff) named Howie, Bettina, and Ty Dyminczyk, a really quiet kid who had just come to Surf

Island Middle from an Eastern European country that we're not sure still exists or not. The one thing we all had in common, besides being friends, was that we hated to be bored and didn't really like to hang around people who did get bored. We had no way of knowing this at the time, but that hike into Pine Hollow forged the core group that later became known as the Outriders.

Way back then we didn't have any gear to climb Eagle Tower, but while we were standing at the base of it, we knew we had just experienced one of the most awesome days ever. We decided to never wait around for cool stuff to happen. We vowed that, from then on, we would make our own cool adventures. (In my blogs I call them expeditions.) So that's why Eagle Tower was so ultra-important to the Outriders. We felt like it sort of *belonged* to us. And now a mining company was going to tear it down.

Somebody, the state legislature, the governor, maybe even the president of the United States, gave permission for this big company to lop off a hunk of Pine Hollow State Forest so that it could dig a humongous open-pit bauxite mine. Mr. Mora, our biology teacher, told us that bauxite is the stuff that aluminum is made of. In about five days the mining company, Amalgamated Bauxite Industries, was going to start dynamiting all around Eagle Tower. By the time they were through, the tower, Sakemwah Hill, and all of our Outrider memories would be gone.

A NEW MYSTERY: BETTINA

I was thinking about all this while I was reloading napkins into the dispensers. I should point out that I don't work at Island Freeze, but I often have to help Kyle with some of the more mundane details of his job in order for him to keep it. My brother is so lax in his assistant manager duties (he is not a fan of the "to do" list) that he is always on the brink of being fired by Mr. Flores, the owner of the Freeze.

I like my brother, but when it comes to food shack middle management, I have to admit, he doesn't try very hard. Kyle claims that he is "conserving his brainpower" for his true calling. Kyle aspires to become the world champion of a multiplayer online game called SporeSlayer. I don't play the game myself, but I think the central idea is that there are these mutant virus spores that transform into gooey, vicious spore-monsters. Apparently, and Kyle is very emphatic about this, SporeSlayer is different from all other first-person shooter games because if you try to kill the spore-monsters in the *wrong* way, they explode into little pieces that grow into even bigger, scarier, and more malevolent spore-monsters. I once mentioned to Kyle that I thought several games employed a variation of this idea. Kyle got so angry at me that he cut me off from free SurfFreezes for a week.

My brother used to be a really respectable surfer (I picked up the sport from him) and an awesome skateboarder. Although he balked at any kind of organized team sport that required mandatory attendance and respect for authority, he was able to throw a football about sixty-five yards. All that ended the day he went over his friend Bodi's house and discovered SporeSlayer. Now Kyle works only to pay for his online gaming fees, eats only to build endurance for SporeSlayer marathons, and sleeps only to dream of ways to defeat mutant viruses. I love my brother, so I back his play, and because of that I do a lot of napkin reloading.

"How's Bettina?" Shelby was now standing beside me helping jam napkins into dispensers. For some reason she was faster and better at it than I was even though I had done it a million times.

"Okay, I guess. We had a close call with that freakishly big horse."

"I'm not talking about that. Something's up with her. Something big."

"Really? She seemed fine."

"As if you'd notice."

"What's *that* supposed to mean?"

Shelby sighed, a deep exasperated sigh, as if I was the thickest person she'd ever had the misfortune to encounter. She does this exasperated-sighing thing quite a lot. Especially with me.

"Fact: Bettina's missed a bunch of school. Fact: She's been sleeping over my house a lot. Fact: I've asked her straight up if something's wrong and she *changed the subject.*"

Shelby was Bettina's best friend and knew her better than anyone. So clearly something major was going on with Bettina. I did a mental rewind of all my conversations and interactions with her to see if I could come up with any useful information. As hard as I tried, I knew before I started that I would come up with nothing. I would never admit this to Shelby, but the truth was, I was entirely capable of missing warning signs. It wasn't because I didn't care about Bettina; it was because Bettina was a girl, and when it comes to what is going on inside of a girl's head, a lot of things confuse me.

The Bonglukiet twins arrived

"What flavor SurfFreezes they got today?" Din said.

"Howie needs a bowl of water," Nar said.

By arriving at this very moment, Din and Nar had helped prove my point. Din, who can eat his body weight in sugar, immediately asked about the Surf-Freezes, and Nar, whose life revolves around his dog, Howie, asked for a water bowl. As Din and Nar are both guys, they just came and said what was on their minds. That's why guys are so easy to figure out. I *think* about surfing and pizza, and I *talk* about surfing and pizza.

But not Shelby and Bettina! You could be talking to Shelby about gymnastics and then you find out the conversation was not about gymnastics at all:

RECENT CONVERSATION WITH SHELBY
Me: How'd your gymnastics thing go?
Shelby: Okay.
Me: You medal?
Shelby: Yeah.
Me: Gold?

Shelby: Uh-huh.
Me: How'd the team do?
Shelby: First.
Me: Cool. When's your next competition?
Shelby: That's just insulting!

Okay, you see that? Things were just breezing along and then WHAMMO! Where did that last comment come from? A few days later it was explained to me by *Bettina (not Shelby)* that Shelby was angry at me because I had mentioned I would *try* to get to her competition. Since I didn't show up, she was disappointed. When I asked about the *next* competition, it made it seem like I was overlooking her *feelings* and didn't care much about her gymnastics at all. Does any of that make sense? Does any of that seem fair?

Here is how that exact same conversation would go with Din (assuming Din was into gymnastics, which he is not):

SIMULATED CONVERSATION WITH DIN

Me: How'd that gymnastics thing go?
Din: Great! I won an individual gold and the team came in first.

Me: Cool.

Din: Hey, how come you didn't come to the competition?

Me: I had to help my dad install a sign.

Din: Oh. Cool.

See how easy that was? Din wondered why I wasn't at the competition, and I got a chance to explain that my dad needed me to help with his work. (My dad owns a sign company.)

Maybe I was all tensed out about this guy/girl communication thing because my friend Bettina was going through something and I had missed it. I turned to Din and Nar and asked, "You guys notice anything weird about Bettina? Shelby thinks something big is happening."

"Didn't notice anything," Nar said.

"Bettina would just spill it if something was wrong, wouldn't she?" Din said.

Shelby did that exasperated sigh thing again. "I might as well be talking to him." Shelby pointed toward Howie, who had just lumbered onto the patio.

Howie is the Galloway of dogs—like I said, 243 pounds (enormous)—and customers seated on the Island Freeze patio backed away toward their cars as if a Bengal tiger had just arrived. Howie always takes the same seat at the Freeze, right below the food window. Mr. Flores has a soft spot for Howie (he likes him much more than Kyle), so he will occasionally toss a hunk of hamburger meat or a hot dog in Howie's direction. When that happens, there is a loud THLOP sound, and the meat never reaches the floor.

Shelby was trying to offend Din, Nar, and me by comparing us to the dog. I guess she views Howie as a "simple" animal that enjoys eating meat, sleeping with his eyes open, and relieving himself prodigiously. It just so happens that Howie is honest and straightforward—guylike. He would never hear the question "When is your next competition?" and respond "That's just insulting!" So by comparing us to Howie, Shelby had given us guys an unintentional compliment. Simple doesn't mean stupid. At least I don't think it does.

I heard the low rumble of a large engine. We all turned to see a vintage convertible Camaro pull into the parking lot. This classic muscle car belonged to Viveca Conroy, Bettina's sister. I immediately swiveled to check out my brother Kyle. Kyle was already at the SurfFreeze dispenser pouring out an extra-large blue raspberry into a plastic Island Freeze souvenir cup. Normally these thirty-two-ounce cups complete with built-in plastic bendy straws cost an additional two dollars with your order. Viveca Conroy hadn't paid for a SurfFreeze since Kyle had been an employee. I watched my brother as he selected the largest and most appetizing mocha cupcake (Viveca's favorite) and put it neatly in a to-go bag.

Bettina entered first, followed by Viveca. Every guy from the age of sixteen to twenty-two in Surf Island, Cedar Cape, and even as far away as Ellistown secretly harbored the ambition of dating Viveca Conroy. Such was the power of her beauty that Kyle would have gladly thrown his PlayStation 3 and his brand-new SporeSlayer: Mutant Carnage game into a wood chipper for a chance to go out with Viveca. It was never going to happen, but guys like my brother dream and hand out free beverages.

I watched the ritual play out. Kyle put the thirty-two-ounce SurfFreeze and the cupcake on the counter. Viveca reached for her purse.

"I got you covered, Viveca," Kyle said.

Viveca flashed her incandescent smile as if this moment had never, ever happened to her before. (In reality, every moment of every day was like this for Viveca.) "Kyle, that is so, so *sweeet* of you."

And Kyle had a reason to live another day.

Then something happened that was so startling, so unprecedented that Kyle and the rest of us could never have anticipated it in a million years.

Viveca turned, lifted her hand, gently pressed it to Bettina's face, and said, "Bets, you call me if you need a ride."

"Thanks, Viv." Bettina said.

"Enjoy yourself today," Viveca said to her sister, and then walked to the parking lot and drove off in her Camaro.

Now I bet you are wondering, "What's so strange about what happened? That doesn't seem odd at all." But that's because you don't know Viveca Conroy very well.

Viveca has one interest: Viveca. Viveca has one thought: "What's in it for me?" Usually if Viveca gave Bettina a ride it was because some deal had been struck. Bettina would have to provide some service that benefited Viveca. The sisters didn't have a bad relationship, just a very practical one. But here in Island Freeze the world had somehow turned upside down.

Shelby looked RIGHT AT ME. This was one of the rare times I knew exactly what was going on in her head because I was thinking the same thing: If Viveca Conroy was being sweet and kind and asking for nothing in return it meant something big was going on with Bettina, and whatever it was, it wasn't good.

Bettina was smart. Wicked smart. She *knew* we had all noticed the ultra-weird conversation with her sister. So when she said, "So what's the plan for Eagle Tower?" we were all supposed to understand that she wasn't going to talk about whatever was going on. See what I mean about this girl stuff? It can drive you crazy.

All eyes turned to me.

"At this moment, I don't have a plan," I said. I don't think my friends had ever heard me utter those words before. It could have been a very glum moment if Wyatt and Ty had not arrived.

"Might have something." Wyatt often dispensed with hellos or appropriately polite greetings.

"Is good," Ty said. Ty and Wyatt made an interesting pair of friends. Ty TOWERED over Wyatt. When he had come from some vague country in Eastern Europe (I don't know much about that area of the world), there was some question as to his exact age. It is possible our friend is four years older than any of us. He is also huge and muscular, with unusually long arms and big hands. Wyatt, on the other hand, can best be described as small and scrappy.

"What's your idea?" I said.

"You better come see it," Wyatt said.

"See what?" Din asked.

"Tough to explain."

"Where is it?" Nar asked.

"The yard," Wyatt said.

SURF ISLAND SALVAGE

The whole group of us and Howie made the ten-minute walk to Sternmetz Marina.

NOTE: It is important for you to remember that name *Sternmetz*. He was a long-ago British naval officer and the Surf Island marina is named after him. Believe it or not the story of Commodore Sternmetz back in the olden days has a lot to do with our Expedition to Pine Hollow, but I'll get to that stuff later. But just remember the name Sternmetz, okay?

At the far end of the marina was Surf Island Salvage. Wyatt's parents, Betty and Morgan Kolbacher, owned and operated this living museum of all things used and nautical.

Wyatt led us along the perimeter of the chain-link fence surrounding the salvage yard. We had decided not to risk entering the yard itself because the vicious, bloodthirsty Kolbacher dog, Saber, a Doberman mix, would be patrolling the rusted piles of marine salvage that was his domain. As long as Wyatt, Betty, or Morgan was present, Saber wouldn't rip any of us to shreds. The reason we didn't dare enter the yard was because Howie was with us.

Saber and Howie have encountered each other before. The moment that Saber locks on to Howie's scent, he begins a low throaty growl that sounds like a lawn mower before you put it in gear. Howie has NO REACTION AT ALL to Saber. Our theory—well, more of a hunch—is that Saber is AFRAID of Howie and tries to act tough around him. What we all wanted to avoid was a confrontation between the two dogs. Howie would come out the victor, but it would be ugly.

So that's why we just stood outside the fence of Surf Island Salvage and looked into the yard at a humongous pile of inky black rubber. You know how when you get a Christmas gift, it might have a ribbon around the box? You know how sometimes you take off the ribbon and sort of fold it over on itself in your hand? Well picture if King Kong got a Christmas gift—and it was wrapped with a five-feet-wide ribbon. That was what this tower of black rubber looked like.

"What is it?" Shelby said.

"An inner tube," Wyatt said.

"That is *one* inner tube?" Din said.

"That's gotta be the biggest inner tube in the world," Nar said.

"That's exactly what it is." Wyatt was smiling.

"Is big," Ty said. This was as enthusiastic as Ty would ever get.

"You're looking at the inner tube of a Caterpillar 797," Wyatt said.

We all let this thought hang there for a moment as if it meant something.

"Are you going to explain?" Shelby was getting frustrated.

"The Caterpillar 797 is a three-hundred-and-sixty-ton-capacity dump truck. Just to give you an idea how big that is, you could fit eight school buses in the truck bed." Wyatt was really in his element;

he loves technical specs. "More important, the tire of a 797 when inflated is *thirteen feet tall*. It is the biggest commercially produced tire on Earth, and that inner tube fits inside of it. My dad salvaged it from a container that fell off a ship."

"Okay, all very fascinating—but how does this help us raise money for Eagle Tower?" Bettina always cuts right to the practical questions.

Wyatt smiled. He had waited for this moment his whole life. He had come up with a plan to rescue an expedition. "Slingshot."

We all stared at Wyatt. Shelby was getting antsy. "Explain."

"We stretch all that rubber between two light posts on the marina, let someone sit on it, and slingshot them out into the water!"

I could tell by the reaction of the other Outriders this suggestion did not ignite a wave of enthusiasm.

"Sounds dangerous," Din said.

"Even if we made it work, how much could we charge?" Nar asked.

Wyatt had hoped for a tidal wave of gratitude and thanks. He didn't expect this tepid response. "I don't know. Five bucks?"

"I don't think anyone will pay five dollars to

become ammunition for a human catapult." Bettina said.

"But . . ." I could tell Wyatt was really disappointed.

I knew how he felt. I'd experienced several big failures with my plans. But Wyatt had succeeded this time, only he didn't know it. "You are a freakish genius!" I said.

Everyone looked at me. Wyatt was really surprised; he had already consigned himself to scrapping his plan.

"We're going to build a giant slingshot?" Shelby seemed confused.

"Nope."

"What we do?" Ty said.

"We inflate it," I said. I have never seen my friends look more puzzled. They didn't know it, but the idea for Tube-O-Topia had been born.

CHAPTER THREE: TUBING

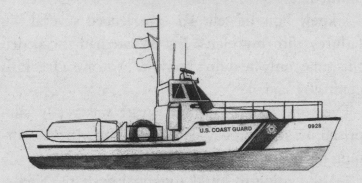

When your bicycle tire gets flat, you simply pull out the old bike pump, you yank it up and down a few times, the tire inflates, and you're good to go. But imagine you have a tire (or inner tube, in this case) that is THIRTEEN FEET TALL and FIVE FEET WIDE and you want to inflate it. The old bike pump in your garage isn't going to cut it.

Also, a bicycle tire, or even an automobile tire, has a standard size valve that fits your old bike pump or even the air compressor at the gas station. The Caterpillar 797 inner tube doesn't have a standard valve. If it did, it would take MONTHS to inflate. The

Caterpillar 797 inner tube had a valve stem that was the size and shape of a can of tennis balls. I have no idea what type of monstrous compressor or inflator connected to that valve, but whatever it was, we didn't have one. So if we were going to inflate the world's largest inner tube, we were going to need some big time help.

TUBE-O-TOPIA

Right about now you might be wondering WHY I wanted to pump air into the humungous black rubber tube. It was because of something I had seen on the Internet: the inflatable banana.

I haven't traveled much farther than fifty miles from my hometown. The only time I've flown in an airplane was on our expedition to Willow Key. But that one experience transformed me. Now all I want to do is travel around the world to cool places. Don't get me wrong, Surf Island is a really great town, but I want to see Mumbai in India, Christchurch in New Zealand, Dar es Salaam in Tanzania, St. Petersburg in Russia, Reykjavik in Iceland, Shanghai in China, Lima in Peru, Saskatoon in Canada, Kuala Lumpur in Malaysia, Verona in Italy, Montevideo in Uruguay, and Kodiak in Alaska (United States). As you probably can tell, I've been on the Internet bookmarking sites of interest. It was on a website for an island in the Caribbean, Anguilla, that I first saw the inflatable banana.

Apparently there are a lot of cool vacation resorts on Anguilla (sort of near Puerto Rico). At one of them I checked out, I saw a picture of a bunch of tourists sitting on top of a thirty-feet-long, bright yellow inflatable banana. This strange ocean watercraft was attached to a long cable and was being towed behind a water-skiing boat. The banana had white rope handles for the riders to hold on to while they straddled the inflatable. All of the tourists looked like they were having the time of their lives cruising around the tropical waters perched on top of a jungle fruit. And here's the most amazing fact: I clicked on the "prices and fees" tab to find out how much it costs to ride the banana—"65 U.S. dollars!"

I counted fourteen people on top of the inflatable. I'm not a whiz at math, but my calculator told me that each banana ride grossed 910 U.S. dollars! Now I know that Surf Island is not a tropical paradise like Anguilla. But we had one thing that no luxury resort in the Caribbean would ever have: the world's largest inner tube. I don't exactly know why people like to be towed behind boats on funny-looking inflatable rafts, but my job wasn't to question the inner workings of the human psyche; my job was to raise money so we could go on the expedition. Somehow, someway, we were going to find a way to inflate the gigantic inner tube, tow it behind a boat, and charge people for the ride.

I had big dreams for Tube-O-Topia. If it worked, it would not only help us get to Eagle Tower, it might become a sustaining source of income for expeditions to come. The Outriders might be able to give up golf-ball farming once and for all.

Obviously people who lived in the Flats were not in the financial position to spend sixty-five bucks to ride atop a ginormous inner tube. We would have to adjust our prices to fit our demographic. But before we could collect even one dollar, there were massive obstacles to overcome:

THE MASSIVE OBSTACLES

1. We had to find a way to inflate the gigantic inner tube.
2. Once inflated, we needed to devise some type of rope handle system so that riders could stay atop the tube.

3. We needed some way to connect a tow cable to the tube.
4. We had to scavenge a boat big and powerful enough to tow a black rubber tube the size of a small home.
5. We had to dig up paying customers.

Like I said, I'm not some freakish engineering genius. I had no idea how to solve some of these tricky technical details on the massive obstacle list. But I knew one person who did: Wyatt's dad, Morgan Kolbacher.

Mr. Kolbacher had spent most of his life in the navy as a chief petty officer. He had been in charge of the maintenance brigade on an aircraft carrier. He could fix or repair ANYTHING that was in or on a boat. Plus he had every part or tool anyone could dream of. Boaters from miles away would arrive at Sternmetz Marina just to seek the technical advice and wisdom of Mr. Kolbacher. But while Mr. Kolbacher was in charge of everything nautical at Surf Island Salvage, Mrs. Betty Kolbacher was in charge of *him*, and Mrs. Kolbacher was angry at the Outriders—particularly me. Mrs. Kolbacher, who stood only a little over five feet tall, should have been number one on the list of massive obstacles.

It's not like I blame Mrs. Kolbacher. She's a really nice lady. Under normal circumstances I think she and Mr. Kolbacher would have loved to help us with our mission. But a few months ago we got in a very tight jam (Shelby's sister, Annabelle, had been kidnapped; long story—see my blog about Blue Cave), and we scavenged the single most important possession of the Kolbachers: their Yamaha GP1300 watercraft. We saved Annabelle, and a lot of people in town considered us heroes for what we did, but Mrs. Kolbacher felt we had "betrayed the Kolbacher family trust" by not coming to them and openly asking for help. They also were really ticked off about the involvement of Wyatt in the whole debacle. Even though we had tried to explain on numerous occasions that the kidnappers insisted that we NOT TELL ANYONE, Mrs. Kolbacher contends—and again, it is hard to argue with her logic—that she and Mr. Kolbacher could have only helped rescue Annabelle. If Tube-O-Topia was to get off the ground, we would have to go through Mrs. Kolbacher.

Wyatt was charged with bringing his mom and dad to the main gate of Surf Island Salvage so we could plead our case. When Mr. and Mrs. Kolbacher arrived, they both set their jaws and put their hands on their hips. Mr. Kolbacher is about six feet six. I could see the U.S. Navy tattoos on his bulging forearms. I don't know much about body language, but I knew our conversation was not starting in a good way.

Mrs. Kolbacher spoke first. "Wyatt told me what you want to do. I'm going to say no and I think you understand why."

"I do, Mrs. Kolbacher."

There was a long silence. My friends looked at me. I think they all expected a lot more from me than "I do, Mrs. Kolbacher." My mind was scrambling for something to say that would convince Wyatt's mother to change her mind, but the problem was I knew we had tricked her and Mr. Kolbacher, and I felt really bad about it.

The Kolbachers have known me since I was born. As a general rule of thumb, if someone has seen you in diapers, it is difficult to surprise or finesse them. They have seen all your moves. My only choice was to go with a super-direct approach.

"If you say no, how does that teach us a lesson?"

"Excuse me?" Mrs. Kolbacher's eyes flashed. She thought I was being *sassy*. That is one tone that will get you nowhere with Mrs. Kolbacher.

"Last time we went around you."

"You did."

"And we're sorry. But now we're doing what you wanted us to do last time—we're coming directly to you for help."

Now it was Mrs. Kolbacher who hesitated. It seemed as if she might be considering that there was truth in what I said.

"We learned our lesson, Mom," Wyatt said.

Mrs. Kolbacher turned and glared at Wyatt. By uttering that one little sentence, he had just ruined everything.

"You know what that sounds like, Wyatt Dean Kolbacher? It sounds like a sassy, young man saying the one thing he thinks his mother wants to hear!"

I couldn't agree with Mrs. Kolbacher more. Here's an important rule of being a kid: Always SHOW your parents you learned your lesson; never, ever, ever SAY, "I have learned my lesson." It sounds insincere and, well, sassy.

Apparently Dean was Wyatt's middle name. Later

we would have to tease him about that. Meanwhile we had to throw in the towel. This fight was over.

For some reason Bettina stepped forward.

"Mr. and Mrs. Kolbacher, this expedition is really, really important to all of us. They are going to tear down Eagle Tower and we would like the chance to explore it one last time. Please help us. It means so much . . . especially to me."

I thought it was very brave of Bettina to make an attempt to sway the Kolbachers. But she didn't know them quite as well as I did. Once Mrs. Kolbacher made up her mind (and Mr. Kolbacher's), it was like a gavel coming down at the end of a trial, the decision was FINAL.

I was just about to turn around and leave when I noticed the weirdest thing. For some reason Mr. and Mrs. Kolbacher's expressions had changed. Sure, Bettina's plea was heartfelt, but I sensed there was something else going on, something beyond my understanding. Mrs. Kolbacher now looked at Mr. Kolbacher. An eternity seemed to pass and then Mr. Kolbacher gave a slight nod. Mrs. Kolbacher now looked back at Bettina.

"Bettina, you promise me you'll keep an eye on this bunch?"

"I do."

"Wyatt, you understand this is a second chance for you and your friends, don't you?"

"Yes, Mom," Wyatt said.

"And no more sassiness!"

"No, Mom."

"Okay, then. I'll lock up Saber in the office."

Mrs. Kolbacher turned and went back into the salvage yard. I understood that she and Mr. Kolbacher were doing this for no one other than *Bettina*. But why? What was going on?

Sometimes adults operate in a secret world all their own.

MORGAN KOLBACHER, MECHANICAL GENIUS

Once Mr. Kolbacher had gotten the thumbs-up from his commander in chief, Mrs. Kolbacher, he kicked into a new gear of industriousness. By nature Wyatt is a "classifier." He likes to order things in his mind. Mr. Kolbacher is a "solver." He enjoys nothing more than looking at a broken piece of machinery for which there haven't been parts available since 1945 and figuring out a way to weld, solder, machine, lathe, plane, laminate, thread, join, bore, counterbore, tap, mill, sink, countersink, drill, or rig a solution.

Remember the list of massive obstacles? Morgan Kolbacher sliced through the obstacles like a Knight Templar with a broadsword.

1. INFLATION: Mr. Kolbacher connected an air hose to an oilless reciprocating tank mount compressor. I know, that is quite a mouthful. Essentially the oilless reciprocating tank mount compressor is a seven-feet-long tank of air with a super-powerful fifty-horsepower engine attached to it. Once you hook up an air hose to it, you basically can create your own hurricane. For instance, if there was some way to tote around this bulky, cumbersome machine, painters could aim it at the shingles of a house and strip all the paint off the wood. Of course it is possible you could blow down a wall of the house at the same time. So you get the idea—Mr. Kolbacher had, as he put it, "just the right tool for the job." Mr. Kolbacher then rooted around in a large pile of salvaged mechanical parts from a sunken fire boat tug and found a "clamp fitting" that enabled him to attach the giant compressor to the world's largest inner tube. Even with a compressor the

size of a rhinoceros, the tube still took forty-five minutes to inflate.

2. ROPE HANDLES: Like most men who spend their lives on or around the sea, Mr. Kolbacher loves knots. He is a knot guy. I've never seen Wyatt's dad happier than when he was slicing hanks of bright yellow three-eighths-of-an-inch polypropylene nylon nautical rope and looping them around the enormous inner tube. Mr. Kolbacher was able to tie a series of "clove hitch" knots so that the ropes stayed in place and then a strange "sheepshank" knot that created a perfect handle for our customers to hold on to.

3. TOW CABLE: Being a marine salvage yard operator, Mr. Kolbacher was all about tow cables. Every single day of every year, Wyatt's dad was towing something on the water. In about twenty minutes, he had created a very sophisticated rig that he claimed would "absorb shock and allow enough play for maneuverability." Obviously none of us stopped to question him about any of this—we simply let Mr. Kolbacher do his thing.

4. THE BOAT: Again, when you need something

done, come to a guy who runs a marine salvage yard. Mr. Kolbacher had a variety of boats. Since Wyatt was going to be our pilot (he knew a freakish amount about nautical charts and navigation), we decided to use the boat Wyatt was most comfortable with: a Boston Whaler Conquest, which was outfitted with twin Mercury seventy-five-horsepower outboard engines. Mr. Kolbacher felt this boat would be sufficiently powerful to tow the humungous inner tube and up to twenty passengers riding atop it. Mr. Kolbacher and Wyatt then took the world's largest inner tube and the Boston Whaler out for a test spin—which went perfectly.

The only massive obstacle that Mr. Kolbacher couldn't help us with was CUSTOMERS. But by the time Wyatt and his dad had returned to the dock we had a line of eager customers waiting to pay twenty dollars apiece to be part of Tube-O-Topia.

You may be wondering how we accomplished this feat without ever leaving Surf Island Salvage. The Bonglukiet twins always had between eight and twelve cousins staying with them at any one time. A few years ago, one of the cousins who had moved to Basking Ridge, New Jersey, (and who was an electronics genius) sent Din and Nar a cellular phone concealed in a Michael Jordan basketball sneaker. We dubbed this device the "bahtphone" because "baht" is the Thai word for shoe. One of the many features of this phone (aside from the fact we never had to pay a bill, don't ask) was that it could send and receive e-mails. So while Mr. Kolbacher was tackling massive obstacles one through four, to solve massive obstacle number five we simply sent a set of strategic e-mails and customers arrived.

You might still be wondering WHY there were so many Surf Islanders interested in being towed on an enormous inner tube and who were willing to come over to Sternmetz Marina on a moment's notice. Well, you should know that all our customers were male high school seniors and their only interest in Tube-O-Topia was that Viveca Conroy had consented to be a passenger on the inaugural ride. Oh, I should mention, my brother Kyle—who graduated high school a year ago—came also.

I had decided that since Viveca had seemed to

be in such an accommodating mood (there's something odd going on, remember?), I would exploit her temporary generosity and use it to the advantage of the Outriders. Normally we would have had to battle through a very tough negotiation, but since we had apparently entered a parallel universe where Viveca was being kind to others, Bettina's older sister seemed almost enthusiastic about coming down to Surf Island Salvage in her bathing suit.

The most complicated part of Tube-O-Topia was trying to keep order among the high school senior guys wanting to ride along with Viveca. Kyle had arrived late (big surprise), so I had to finesse it for him to get on the ride (the brother code). We almost had fistfights break out among the remaining customers. Only Mr. Kolbacher's enormous size and scary-looking navy tattoos allowed us to keep order.

Finally we got Viveca, Kyle, and eighteen very eager seniors mounted on top of the world's largest inner tube. This would have been virtually impossible if it hadn't been for a rope ladder that Mr. Kolbacher had rigged that enabled the customers to climb atop the black rubber whale. Mr. Kolbacher insisted that everyone had to wear life jackets (navy regulations), so all twenty passengers were decked out in bright orange vests.

Shelby, Bettina, Ty, Din, Nar, Wyatt, and I climbed aboard the boat. Of course Howie had to be in the center of the action, so he got comfortable in a shady spot just inside the Boston Whaler's cabin. As I had climbed aboard, I'd noticed the name of the Kolbacher boat. It was called the *Bitsy Betsy*. Wyatt explained that Bitsy was Mr. Kolbacher's pet name for his wife. I had a tough time imagining someone other than Mr. Kolbacher having the guts to call Mrs. Kolbacher "Bitsy." But I didn't have time to let my mind drift to other ports. I had three hundred and sixty dollars in my pocket (Viveca and Kyle got the ride for free), and the Bitsy Betty was pulling out into the open ocean. Tube-O-Topia was officially underway.

WYATT'S WILD RIDE

For twenty minutes I was a genius. The Boston Whaler Conquest and its twin seventy-five-horse-power Mercs effortlessly pulled the world's largest inner tube and the twenty passengers out to sea. The *Bitsy Betsy* was heading south in the direction of Rocky Point Beach (where I do all of my surfing), the sun sparkled on the foamy green sea, and I could feel the wad of twenty-dollar bills in the back pocket of my jeans. Some days plans don't turn out well. On other days, they turn out pretty much as you'd expect. But on certain rare days, your plans take on the qualities of dreams.

I looked back at the Caterpillar 797 inner tube, which was slick and glistening with salt water. I saw the happy faces of Viveca, Kyle, and eighteen contented, paying customers. I then looked over toward my friend Wyatt at the helm of the *Bitsy Betsy*, his smile could not be contained on his face. Shelby, Bettina, Din, and Nar were content to catch some rays, and even Howie had his head up above his paws and seemed to be inhaling the fresh aroma of brine and sunscreen.

Maybe our attention was too focused on the giant inner tube. We were near the south end of Surf Island, right around Sanctuary Bay. None of us even *saw* the water-skiers. Had it been just ONE lone water-skier, what I'm about to tell you would never have happened. But as fate would have it, the Cedar Cape International Waterskiing Championship was under way. I'm not sure if you know anything about waterskiing, but the boats GO FAST, really fast. And championship water-skiers go faster than just normal everyday water-skiers. That's why the boats were on top of us before we knew what had happened.

If the *Bitsy Betsy* were at the center of a watch dial and headed toward twelve o'clock, the armada of waterskiing boats (and champion water-skiers) was coming RIGHT AT US from the ten o'clock position. I noticed that some of the boat captains were realizing that they had a Boston Whaler Conquest directly in front of them, and if that wasn't bad enough, it was towing the world's largest inner tube with twenty people sitting on top of it.

Here's something important you need to know about Wyatt: He's an awesome guy, a loyal friend, but to be honest, he's not really good under pressure. When you surf, you learn that when things start moving fast, you have to find a way to get calm or things will go from bad to ultra-bad in a hurry. Wyatt reacted like a lot of people would with about forty waterskiing boats about to ram the hull of their dad's boat: He YANKED the wheel of the *Bitsy Betsy* HARD TO THE RIGHT. That might not have been so bad, but for some reason Wyatt's instincts told him to go FULL THROTTLE, as if to OUTRUN the waterskiing armada.

So many bad things happened that it is hard to keep them all straight.

When a powerboat makes a tight turn at a high speed, there is a very good chance that it will tip over. The same principal applies to a car, but a boat rolls very quickly and with almost no warning. Luckily we had so much ballast (thank you, Howie) that Wyatt succeeded in making what amounted to a racing boat turn. The only small problem was that he completely neglected to remember the Caterpillar 797 inner tube with twenty passengers that we were towing.

Mr. Kolbacher had come up with a very stable towing rig. He had fastened TWO cables to the *Bitsy Betsy*, one on the port aft (left rear) and one on the starboard aft (right rear). These two lines met at a point twenty feet behind the boat and then were connected to a single cable that towed the gigantic inner tube. The simplest way to describe what the towing rig looked like is the letter *Y*. But no towing rig was designed to withstand a racing boat turn. One of the top parts of the *Y* was sliced clean through by the outboard engine's propeller. So now there was no *Y* anymore—the world's largest inner tube was connected by a *single cable* to the *Bitsy Betsy*.

The other downside of the POWER TURN, as we would call it, was that the Tube-O-Topia customers found themselves turning at high speed. Not only did the tube almost tip over, but the nose of it dove down as a result of the sudden increase in acceleration. Rooster tails of sea spray were now dousing Viveca, Kyle, and the eighteen high school seniors. It was as if twenty people were being subjected to the high-speed nozzle of a fire hose.

Again, we might have been able to weather this storm if the fishing boats hadn't been in the way. Two trawlers fully laden with many tons of red snappers were now directly in our path. I guess the fishermen had a really big afternoon, because the nets dangling from the booms were bursting with fish.

Remember that watch dial? The waterskiing boats had been coming from the ten o'clock position. By making the POWER TURN, Wyatt had now pointed us toward four o'clock, which was the exact position of the fishing boats. We were seconds away from RAMMING one of the trawlers.

Another thing you should know about boats is

that they don't just STOP. There are no *brakes* on a boat. If you are moving at forty knots and just turn off the outboard engine, you will eventually slow down, but not for a long time. Had Wyatt just cut the engines, we would have crashed into the fishing trawler. So Wyatt did the ONLY THING he could do, he made a quick correction (jerked the wheel again) and ROCKETED across the bow of the lead fishing trawler.

Again, on a normal day Wyatt would have averted disaster. The *Bitsy Betsy* easily cleared the bow of the lead trawler with about three feet to spare. But remember, we were towing the humongous inner tube and the twenty now SCREAMING passengers.

Two bad things happened at once: The big rubber inner tube SMACKED into the bow of the trawler. The inner tube managed to absorb the blow, but it was sent ricocheting across the water. I could actually see the white knuckles of all the passengers as they were death-gripping the polypropylene sheepshead knots. Oh, the second bad thing that happened: The SMASH of the inner tube against the fishing boat caused the nets to rip off the booms and THOUSANDS OF RED SNAPPERS were released back into the water.

I guess a full catch of red snapper is really valuable, because this made the fishing captain REALLY, INTENSELY ANGRY. When someone gets that upset, they tend to lash out. I saw the fishing captain accelerate, as if to chase after us. One of the deckhands took out what looked to be a HARPOON. I guess the thought was that the enormous inner tube had caused them to lose all their fish, so they were going to vent their frustration by PUNCTURING the inner tube.

Their plans were thwarted immediately because Wyatt's second POWER TURN had brought us on a collision course for Goat's Neck Bridge. Surf Island isn't technically an island; it is more of a peninsula. The reason I say "more of a peninsula" is that the narrow strip of land (Goat's Neck) that connects Surf Island to the mainland is more of a marshy, fetid, swamp than a real hunk of land. This geographical anomaly is what saved all of our lives.

The *Bitsy Betsy* PLOWED straight into Goat's Neck. The good thing about outboard engines is that they kick up if they hit something. Both engines bucked upward on the transom as the bow of our boat made contact with land. But since Goat's Neck is so marshy, the *Bitsy Betsy* actually SHOT ACROSS the narrow strip of gunky cattail reeds and broke through into SURF ISLAND LAGOON on the far side of the bridge! The outboards (still running full throttle) dropped back down into the water and powered us forward. I was so elated we hadn't crashed that even I forgot about the ginormous inner tube behind us. Somehow the tow cable held and the whole inner tube with all twenty passengers MOWED through the cattails like some type of monstrous WEED WHACKER clearing a swath of flattened cattails behind it.

That's when the *Bitsy Betsy* almost hit the buoy. Wyatt had made a common mistake of boaters. He was looking behind him (concerned about the Tube-O-Topia customers) and was not keeping an eye on the channel marker buoy. Some buoys are big and most often they are made of metal, so it is best to avoid smashing into them. Wyatt did yet a THIRD POWER TURN and managed to just nip the Boston Whaler against the buoy. But the world's largest inner tube hit it full on.

The black rubber tube was so slick and slippery that

the buoy went UNDER IT. The half-submerged buoy acted like a waterskiing ramp. The Caterpillar 797 tube now became airborne. I'm not deeply scientific, so I don't understand any of the laws of physics that caused this to happen, but the speed and the wind resistance of the airborne tube caused it to twist sideways.

I have to give those customers credit—they hung on. Even when the inner tube was being dragged ON ITS SIDE. If you were on shore or on Goat's Neck Bridge watching the disaster unfold, it would have looked like the world's largest tire was rolling upright across the water with Tube-O-Topia passengers dangling off the sides like curtain tassels.

Wyatt tried to cut the engines but he became distracted by the EXPLOSION.

The lagoon area just on the other side of the bridge isn't used much by boaters because there are a lot of sunken pier pilings and old pieces of the original wooden Goat's Neck Bridge. Most probably the buoy that we hit was marking the channel to alert boaters of all these dangers. The bottom line was, the world's largest inner tube struck something that caused it to POP.

You remember how much compressed air was inside of it? Well, when all that air rushed OUT of a constrained space, it had a great deal of force. There was a sort of WHOOSHING sound and we watched as Viveca, Kyle, and the eighteen other high school seniors were SLINGSHOTTED high into the air. (Remember Wyatt's original idea for the inner tube?) They flew for quite some distance before they came splashing down. For a brief instant it looked as if it was raining *people*.

Immediately Wyatt jerked the boat around, but he had the presence of mind to reduce the throttle. He had to be very careful that we wouldn't run the boat over the survivors. We watched heads popping up one by one all over the water. Mr. Kolbacher's insistence on the lifejackets was now the greatest suggestion in the history of mankind. The vests made it easy for all of our passengers to bob safely in the water.

Without being asked, Shelby and Bettina were trying to get a head count to see if everyone was above water and no one was below. Shelby, who is wicked fast at math, determined everyone was alive and treading water.

We became aware of another sound: a huge diesel turbine engine. I turned to see a U.S. Coast Guard forty-four-feet motor lifeboat heading toward our location. If anyone from Tube-O-Topia had been injured, the arrival of the Coast Guard would be welcome news. But we Outriders were well acquainted with the Coast Guard, and they were well acquainted with us. Put it this way: They did not return our feelings of respect and admiration.

Ty, Din, and Nar were busy reaching over the sideboards and helping the high school guys into the boat. Shelby pointed to a spot off the aft and I saw something I would remember for the rest of my life. Viveca Conroy had my brother Kyle in a lifesavers hold (hand cupped under his chin, his body resting atop of hers) and she was sidekicking him toward the *Bitsy Betsy*! All the rest of the high school guys had been blown off the giant inner tube and landed safely in the water. But not Kyle. Somehow he must have landed in a belly flop and gotten the wind knocked out of him. Kyle was finally in the arms of the woman of his dreams—and he was unconscious.

By the time the Coast Guard motor lifeboat pulled alongside the *Bitsy Betsy*, we had everyone safe and accounted for. The Coast Guard commander—his name tag read LT. CORKIN—called to us over a bull-horn, "Ahoy!"

He actually said, "Ahoy!" I don't know why he was using a bullhorn; he was only fifteen feet away from us.

"Hi, Lieutenant," I said.

"What the heck happened out here?"

I didn't have the strength to describe the onslaught of professional water-skiers, the chase by hostile fishermen, the plunge through the reeds under Goat's Neck Bridge, the collision with the buoy, the popping of the world's largest inner tube, or the rescue of Kyle, so I just said, "We got it under control, Lieutenant."

"Under control? Is that what you call it?"

I didn't say a word. I didn't want to be sassy to a Coast Guard officer.

"That kid all right?"

He was pointing at my unconscious brother, whose head was resting in Viveca's lap.

I watched as a Coastie carrying an orange tackle box full of medical gear started to come forward so that he could board the *Bitsy Betsy*.

I knelt down next to my brother to check his injuries. As I hovered over him, HE WINKED AT ME. It was at that moment I realized that Kyle was using a lot more of his "brainpower" than I have ever given him credit for. Kyle stirred as if "coming to" and looked up at Viveca.

"Dude, you saved my life," he said to her.

Viveca blushed. She had never known that there was a hero locked inside of her.

I called to Lieutenant Corkin, "He's going to be okay, Lieutenant! Just had the wind knocked out of him!"

"Took my breath away," Kyle said while staring up at Viveca.

"You there, captain of the *Bitsy Betsy*!" The Lieutenant was now addressing Wyatt.

Even though Wyatt knew he was going to get yelled at, he felt good that someone had called him "captain."

"You are never to tow that big tube thing again, is that clear?"

It was a pretty silly thing for Lieutenant Corkin to say. The Tube-O-Topia tube was now just a large misshapen blob of rubber floating on the surface of the lagoon. The polypropylene ropes dangled from it like bright yellow octopus tentacles. No one would ever be riding atop the tube again.

But Wyatt was smart enough to say, "Yes, sir."

"You're Morgan Kolbacher's boy, right?"

Mr. Kolbacher was well known by all the Coasties. He fixed their boats and was a local legend in the nautical circles.

"Yes, sir." Wyatt had perked up. Being Morgan Kolbacher's son had some street cred out on the water.

"I'm going to have a talk with your dad. Unless he's out here with you, I don't EVER want to see you piloting a boat again. You're not to be trusted."

Wyatt didn't have anything to say. I knew exactly what he was thinking. Just when he had worked so hard to get back inside the Kolbacher family trust, he would be thrown out again.

"Are we clear on that, young man?"

"Clear, sir."

"Everyone all right?" Lieutenant Corkin yelled down to all of us on the Boston Whaler.

"Yes, sir," twenty-seven voices said in unison with the same lack of enthusiasm.

The motor lifeboat pulled away. I was actually sorry to see them go as I knew that now I would be facing twenty angry Tube-O-Topia customers, eighteen demanding their twenty dollars back. There would be no expedition and very little joy among the Outriders.

One of the high school seniors, I think his name was Jon Messeri, said, "Hey, Cam."

Okay, here it was. I reached into my jeans for the money.

"YOU GOTTA FIX THAT BIG BLACK DONUT THING! WE NEED TO GO AGAIN, DUDE!"

All eighteen high school seniors CHEERED.

Even Kyle gave me the thumbs-up. "It rocked," my brother said.

"Did you hit your head?" I said, not expecting a compliment from my brother.

"That was better than SporeSlayer," Kyle said.

I felt like I had just won the world cup of surfing.

"What's SporeSlayer?" Viveca said.

My brother smiled, perhaps the biggest smile of his life. "Someday I'll show you."

Tube-O-Topia had been a strange success and we

could now afford to buy climbing gear and go to Eagle Tower. Maybe we all wouldn't have been so elated if we had known where our climbing gear would take us.

CHAPTER FOUR: TREKKING

Let me get one thing out of the way. None of us Outriders were experienced rock climbers, but we did know the basics. Rock climbing is not a sport you might associate with Surf Island. The gear is expensive, and unless you have a really experienced instructor, it's not something you can pick up on your own. There's too much technical stuff to know and a whole lot of bad things can happen if you decide to "wing it." If you had no surfing experience but decided to charge out into little baby waves with a surfboard, not too many bad things can happen. Sure, you can bonk yourself in the head with your own board, but when you fall, you fall in *water*. You try scaling a face of vertical rock without knowing what you are doing—I don't even want to explain what could and *would* happen.

The only reason any of us know the first thing about rock climbing is because our biology teacher, Mr. Mora, loves the sport. He somehow convinced the school board to let him turn a brick wall on the side of Surf Island Middle School into a climbing wall. Mr. Mora didn't have tons of money, but he was part of a rock-climbing club, and all the members donated a few handholds and belay cables, and within a few months we all had the basics down. For safety reasons, Mr. Mora forbade any student to use the wall during nonschool hours, but we felt that rule applied to other kids, not the Outriders.

So we could all set up a harness, do some basic protection (remember anchors?), climb, and rappel (descend using the rope). We actually had much more training than we needed to make the ascent up the side of Eagle Tower and rappel to the bottom. The climb has an almost zero degree of technical difficulty. But, because it is rock climbing, we needed gear, and that's why I headed over to

Sportco Giant Lots Discount when they opened at eight a.m.

Our Tube-O-Topia profits more than covered what we required. Since Eagle Tower is only forty feet tall, we just had to buy a bunch of protection (anchors), a harness, and some climbing rope. Luckily we didn't need truly technical gear, because it costs major bucks and our income potential had disappeared—the world's largest inner tube was not going to be carrying passengers again anytime soon.

Sportco Giant Lots Discount sells sporting goods in BULK. For instance, if you wanted to buy a soccer ball, you would have to buy a CARTON of *twelve soccer balls.* This is really great when you are the coach of a soccer team and not so great if you are a kid wanting to kick the ball around in your backyard.

Sportco Giant Lots Discount had some decent climbing gear (for our needs, anyway), but it came in mass quantities. For instance we needed climbing rope. (Rock climbers call this a static line.) Sportco Giant Lots Discount sold climbing rope in lengths of FIVE HUNDRED FEET. This would be fantastic if you were climbing the south face of El Capitan in Yosemite, but it was a bit much for a forty-foot tower. If we were forced to abide by Sportco Giant Lots Discount's bulk policy, we would never have been able to afford to purchase our gear. But we have an inside contact. Her name is Olivia Ray.

Olivia is one of the members of Mr. Mora's rock-climbing club. She's got a mop of really frizzy light brown hair that she tucks under a baseball cap that says "CLIMBERS ROCK!" I'm not positive, but I think she sort of crushes on Mr. Mora. Mr. Mora isn't movie-star good-looking or anything, but he *really* cares about stuff like ecosystems, ozone depletion, and baby condors. So if someone cares about our planet (like Olivia Ray), it would follow that they are going to like Mr. Mora because he considers himself (and all of his students) guardians of "every living thing." So when Mr. Mora called Olivia and told her I would be heading over to Sportco Giant Lots Discount to see her, she rolled out her own version of the red carpet.

Sportco Giant Lots Discount is part of a large chain of warehouse sporting goods stores (locations in twelve states). They have a strict policy to sell only bulk packages. However, if a box is opened or damaged in shipping, store employees do have some latitude to sell off individual items from those boxes. Obviously the store would prefer to "move the merchandise" rather than go through the expense and bother of returning it. By the time I had arrived at Sportco Giant Lots Discount, Olivia Ray had discovered that several boxes of climbing gear had mysteriously fallen off an improperly loaded forklift. Because the boxes of climbing rope, carabiners, and harnesses were now ripped open, Olivia, always abiding by store policy, was able to sell me just what I needed.

By the way, I thought it was best to go alone to see Olivia because it might look very CONSPICUOUS and SUSPICIOUS if seven kids and a 243-pound mastiff were all buying SINGLE items rather than cartons. No one would notice *one* kid carrying some climbing gear toward the registers.

"Thanks, Ms. Ray," I said.

"Olivia. Just lucky for you those boxes were damaged."

It was hard for me not to smile.

"How's Peter?" Olivia said.

She meant Mr. Mora; Peter is his first name. "He's okay."

"He's more than 'okay,' Cam." Now Olivia was smiling. "Oh, I had a couple of old lids lying around. Mind wearing them while you're getting vertical?" Olivia handed me a bunch of climbing helmets.

"No problem," I said. I sensed Mr. Mora watching over our expedition from behind the scenes, pulling strings like a master puppeteer.

The walkie-talkie I had gotten from Din crackled to life.

"The ducks are on the pond. Repeat. The ducks are on the pond. Over." Wyatt felt it mandatory to use walkie-speak and secret code whenever possible.

Olivia Ray started to laugh. "You kids run a tight operation."

I shrugged. I realize to the outside world we Outriders are not the most normal bunch of kids. "Ms. . . . Olivia, I have to go."

"I know. The ducks are on the pond."

RETURN TO THE LAGOON

The "ducks" Wyatt referred to were actually Old Town Tripper canoes, but I'll explain about them in a second.

If you ever check out a map of Surf Island, you'll

notice it is shaped like a football. The *south* end of the football has a thin strip of land connecting it to the mainland. (Remember Goat's Neck?) Pine Hollow State Forest is *west* of Surf Island, much closer to the *north* end of the football. There are only two ways to get there, and both presented problems:

First way to get to Pine Hollow: CAR

Problem: We did not have a car or driver's licenses.

Second way to get to Pine Hollow: BOAT

Problem: The U.S. Coast Guard (mostly Lieutenant Corkin) had banned us from using the Kolbacher Boston Whaler.

But no one said anything about canoes. Many members of the Bluffs Yachting and Beach Club (yes, it is affiliated with the Bluffs Country Club) own canoes. Really awesome canoes. All of these top-of-the-line watercraft just sit in the boathouse getting cleaned and tended to once a month by the boat staff of the club. I have never seen one member (they are all really ancient) out in the lagoon paddling his Old Town canoe. It was just never going to happen. Canoeing is much more strenuous than drinking cocktails in the lounge, so we never worried if we had to scavenge some canoes for an expedition—nobody would miss them.

We selected the Old Town Trippers because they can carry a lot of gear. We weren't really loaded down with that much stuff—we were mostly loaded down with Howie. Just a word of advice if you are embarking on an expedition: Mastiff planning can be difficult and time consuming; allot extra man-hours.

The shortest crossing of the lagoon was from the northern tip of the Surf Island football. A half-hour paddle would put us at Shady Cove, an abandoned picnic ground, where we knew of a great place to hide our scavenged canoes. From there it would be a four-hour hike to Eagle Tower. Our plan was to explore the tower, camp out overnight, and return the next day.

You would think our parents would have freaked out that we were camping overnight with no adult super-vision, but we had done this type of thing before. Here is the logic behind our parents' thinking:

1. There were seven Outriders—safety in num-bers.
2. We knew Pine Hollow State Forest—we con-sidered it our backyard.

3. We were bringing Howie—no explanation necessary.

So our fleet of canoes set off from the northern tip of Surf Island. High up on the Bluffs, two hundred feet above us, we could see the distinctive roof line of Falcon's Lair. Mr. Thorpe seemed to have an eerie knowledge of the activities of the Outriders; I wondered if he was peering through one of his many telescopes at this very moment. It is even possible that one of these Old Town Tripper canoes belonged to him. I hoped not.

Din and Nar were paddling the largest canoe. Howie was comfortably resting along the beam (widest part of the vessel), between them. This was problematic as Din and Nar are small and Howie is huge. So we all knew the pace of the crossing was going to be set by the Bonglukiet boat.

Ty and Wyatt were paddling together. This created another nautical problem. In a canoe, the strongest paddler should sit in front. So obviously Ty was going to be in the bow of the boat. But Ty is MUCH BIGGER and STRONGER than Wyatt. So for each one of Ty's powerful strokes, Wyatt had to compensate with *three* of his own. Needless to say, the Ty/Wyatt canoe spent a lot of time zigzagging across the lagoon.

Shelby, Bettina, and I were in the third canoe. You would think that the additional weight of three people would slow the boat down, but don't forget, that third person is paddling. I know it wasn't supposed to be a race but Shelby, Bettina, and I RIPPED across the lagoon. We made it to Shady Cove, hid our boat, and still had to wait a full fifteen minutes for the rest of the fleet to pull ashore.

Once everyone was ashore we stowed the remaining boats, put on our day packs, and began our trek into Pine Hollow.

THE HOLLOW AND ITS SECRETS

The Hollow (that's what we call it) is wild. There are thousands of acres of pine trees, just two small campgrounds, and a tiny ranger station with one park ranger. Not a lot of tourists come to the Hollow, only hard-core campers who are searching for a rugged outdoor experience.

There are very few paved roads in Pine Hollow. The main way to get through the dense forest is on fire trails. We were setting out on the Sakemwah Trail headed toward Eagle Tower.

Every time I come back to the Hollow, I am reminded of how ultra-awesome and beautiful it is. The pines are so tall that it is perpetually shady. No matter what time of day you are hiking, it feels like dusk. Even if it is a hundred degrees in Surf Island, the temperature of Pine Hollow is always cool. You have to wear a sweatshirt even at midday.

I love the smell. Mr. Mora says that our sense of smell is the most primal of our senses. Here in the Hollow, the crisp scent of the pines makes you feel taller and more alive. I tried to imagine how the Sakemwah Indians felt when they first walked into this forest. They probably thought they'd like to stay here and never leave. At least that's how I felt.

The forest floor and the fire trails are carpeted with a thick plushy mat of pine needles. This makes the Hollow one of the quietest places on earth. When you hike on the pine needles, you can't even hear your own footsteps. I notice that my friends and I whisper whenever we come here. It's almost like it would be rude to make loud noises. We didn't want to insult the peacefulness of the forest. Maybe that is why, two hours into our trek, it was so easy to hear the diesel engines.

"What is that?" I whispered to Wyatt.

"Something big," Wyatt whispered back.

"Whatever it is, the sound is getting *closer*." Shelby had to speak a little louder as the engine noise was increasing.

I didn't have to say a word. All of us left the wide fire trail and cut into the woods. We could run as fast as we wanted; the carpet of pine needles muffled any sounds we could make, and by this time the diesel engine noise was almost deafening. We found a fallen pine tree and all ducked behind it. Nar (who fancies himself a dog whisperer) had to command Howie into a down position to conceal the massive dog behind the log.

Here is the strangest thing about what we saw next: None of us had ever seen the monstrous machine that was now on the Sakemwah Trail, but we knew exactly what it was. Well, that is not truly accurate; we had all seen the *inner tube* of the gigantic truck in front of us. It was a three-story-high behemoth DUMP TRUCK. There was a STAIRWAY on the front of the truck for the driver to climb to get up to the cab, which was level with the tops of some of the pines. The gargantuan truck was so WIDE that it was knocking over pine trees that lined the fire trail, leaving only jagged stumps in its wake. I saw Din using the camera in the Bahtphone to snap pictures.

Until now the Caterpillar 797 had been some sort of mythic vehicle that existed only in our imaginations, but now the 360-ton-capacity dump truck was invading the heart of the unspoiled forest—our unspoiled forest.

I don't think it was a coincidence Mr. Kolbacher had salvaged a Caterpillar 797 inner tube from a container that fell in the ocean. Clearly there was a massive dump truck in the area and it needed supplies. But why was it trundling down Sakemwah Trail five days ahead of schedule?

Behind the world's largest dump truck was a line of support vehicles: two diesel-fuel tankers, a bunch of road graders, bulldozers, and pickup trucks. You would have thought that when the caravan passed, the diesel engine noise would have died down. But it didn't. Something else was coming up the road. Even Howie lifted his muzzle above the fallen pine tree to take a look. What we saw was so freakishly huge that the Caterpillar 797 instantly became the *second* biggest thing in the forest. It wasn't even close; this was the hugest, most gigantic man-made vehicle that could have possibly been constructed since the beginning of time.

It was a shovel. It moved along on treads (like a battle tank) instead of tires. The mechanical creaking of the treads sounded like an invading army had launched an assault, shattering the silence of the wood. Remember Wyatt telling us that eight school buses could fit into the bed of the Caterpillar 797? The shovel on the front of this vehicle was big enough to LOAD those buses onto the Caterpillar. The top of the shovel crane was about EIGHT STORIES HIGH. It was so much taller than the biggest pines that it actually blotted out the sun. We were enveloped in a deep, inky black shadow as the shovel passed. Even in the dim light we all could read the lettering on the side of the huge vehicle: AMALGAMATED BAUXITE INDUSTRIES.

I could tell my friends were as confused as I was, but before we could utter even a single thought, a cat jumped into Bettina's arms. Obviously when you are in the woods and an animal jumps on you, even an animal the size of a cat, you are FREAKED OUT. Bettina was really rattled and scared, but not as frightened as the cat. It was trying to hide in Bettina's thick curly hair. As you know, Bettina is really good with animals, but she couldn't get this cat to calm down.

"It's probably afraid of Howie," Nar said to Bettina.

Cats are completely off Howie's radar. Howie wasn't looking at the cat at all. He was looking behind us.

"Is not Howie," Ty said. He then pointed in the direction Howie was looking—at a BEAR.

When you watch nature programs, bears look really cute and cuddly. But when there is nothing but thirty yards of open ground between you and a bear, they don't look as friendly. This was a black bear, which is supposed to be shyer and less dangerous than a brown one, but this bear was doing something you don't want to see any bear doing: standing on its hind legs. He was making himself BIG for a reason.

Almost every person walking the earth has heard this tidbit of information: *If you ever encounter a bear in the woods, play dead.* Here's the problem with that info. It is never, ever going to happen. What really happens when you see a bear is that your brain

FREEZES AND STOPS SENDING SIGNALS TO YOUR MUSCLES. What you do is STARE AT THE BEAR and HOPE HE DOESN'T COME AFTER YOU. Sure, random thoughts rattle around in your frozen brain—thoughts like "RUN" or "SHOUT" or "PICK UP A BRANCH." But no matter how many of these thoughts are bouncing around, what you do is NOTHING.

I looked down at Howie. He was now sitting up and staring at the bear with his head cocked in the "what's that?" position. His hackles (the hairs on the back of his neck) were not standing up. This was a good sign. If Howie didn't sense imminent danger, things might not be as catastrophic as they seemed.

The bear had his nose tilted up in the air and seemed to be sniffing. But he wasn't really looking in our direction—he was looking toward the behemoth strip-mining shovel that was so heavy, it SHOOK THE GROUND as it rumbled down the fire trail. We Outriders had never seen anything like it, so it stands to reason the bear was confused as well. I was scared of the bear, but to be honest, the bear also seemed afraid. I think the bear was wondering what type of monster was entering his forest—a predator he couldn't possibly compete with. As soon as the shovel disappeared from view, the bear got down on all fours, looked briefly in our direction, and then bounded off into the darkness of the pines. For those of you who think bears lumber around in slow motion, take note: They move a lot faster than you can imagine.

"Oh. My. God." Shelby was actually shaking.

That was all any of us could manage to say. I heard a rapid POUNDING sound and then realized it was the jackhammering of my own heart.

The moment the bear had left the vicinity, the stray cat poked his head through the protective curtain of Bettina's hair. The cat was sleek and had the exact coloring and markings of a tiny leopard. I'm not really a cat person. Don't get me wrong, I like cats, and will even let Shelby's tabby, Vanilla, sit on my lap for hours. But remember my problem figuring out what goes on in girl's minds? I have that same problem with cats. I'll be petting Vanilla and she'll be purring. Then, out of nowhere, she'll bare her claws, start hissing, and scratch my hand to ribbons. What is that about?

"Ocicat," Shelby said.

"Excuse me?" I said.

"That's an ocicat. It's a purebred." Shelby knew cats in the same way Bettina knew horses.

"What's it doing way out here?" Nar said.

"Um, guys, do we want to talk about what we just saw? Those mining trucks?" I was getting very impatient.

"We have to take the cat with us. We can't leave her out here alone," Shelby said.

Apparently the cat was a she.

"She doesn't have a collar." Bettina was now rubbing her fingers under the ears of the cat; it really seemed to enjoy it.

"Excuse me? Hello? Did anyone see the humungous mining trucks? Can we focus on that for a minute?"

Bettina opened the top of her day pack and put the cat inside. The cat put its paws on the top lip of the open pack and seemed very content to be a passenger.

"She's so cute! We have to name her," Shelby said.

Okay, we just witnessed a caravan of the world's most voracious mining equipment and came face-to-face with a black bear, but Shelby and Bettina felt it was time to name a stray cat.

"Ki," Shelby said.

Since it wasn't a name that anyone recognized, we all waited for an explanation.

"It's Japanese. It means energy. Ai-*ki*-do."

Aikido is the martial art Shelby studies. It's not famous like kung-fu or karate, but it still works really well. I have several bruises to prove it.

"Ki! I love that!" Bettina said.

"Okay, the cat has a name. Do you mind if we talk about THOSE TRUCKS!"

"You don't have to shout," Shelby said to me.

"You'll scare Ki," Bettina said.

"I thought they weren't supposed to start digging the mine for five more days," Wyatt said.

I tried to control my volume. "Yes, that was the point I was trying to make."

"What's going on, then?" Din was scrolling through the pictures he had taken on the Baht-phone.

"That's what I'm wondering," I said.

"We should follow them. See what's going on." Nar was scratching Howie's tummy.

"Is no good," Ty said, but knew no one was going to listen to his warning.

We Outriders are a curious bunch, and you know

what they say about curiosity—that it killed the cat. Well, in our case, it turned out the cat saved our lives. But you need to know a bunch of stuff before that makes sense.

CHAPTER FIVE: DISCOVERING

It is extremely easy to follow an eight-story strip-mining shovel and a 360-ton capacity dump truck. You could be deprived of four of your five senses and be able to do it. You could follow the diesel smell just with your nose. You could track the eight-story shovel with only your eyes. You could lock on to the thunderous rumble of the engines with just your ears, and your sense of touch would direct you toward the seismic vibrations created by the massive machinery. I haven't figure out how you could use your sense of taste, but you get the idea.

Right at the base of Sakemwah Hill, the pine-needle path of Sakemwah Trail becomes rocky and steep. The path winds around boulders and huge stone formations and ends atop Sakemwah Hill at a mesa of rock that locals call the Table. Shelby told me that *mesa* is the Spanish word for "table," so this makes a great deal of literal sense. Eagle Tower sits almost in the center of the Table. I don't know much about heavy mining equipment, but I knew there was no way for any of the vehicles to climb Sakemwah Hill. So it was no surprise to any of us that all the vehicles veered off on another fire trail called Mingwa Trail. Wyatt informed us that Mingwa was the supreme chief of the Sakemwah. In the language of the Sakemwah, Mingwa meant "water chief," but that's all the history that Wyatt could produce on the subject. Anyway, Mingwa Trail led down into a valley below Sakemwah Hill. That's where we saw the mining camp.

Even Wyatt didn't know anything about the rules and regulations governing mining companies, but we had all read the article in the *Ellistown Chronicle* about Amalgamated Bauxite Industries getting permission to build a bauxite mine in Pine Hollow State Forest. This was the article that first alerted us that if we ever wanted to see Eagle Tower again, we would have to hurry and plan our expedition. Here is a snippet of the article:

Ellistown Chronicle

OPEN PIT OF DESPAIR
By Laura Moss

Despite vigorous opposition at the local level, Amalgamated Bauxite received a mineral rights lease to begin no sooner than Sept 24th. The mayors of Cedar Cape and Ellistown and the city manager of Surf Island vowed that they would be continuing their fight to deny the mineral lease. Hal Sadoff, Surf Island City Manager, stated that the struggle would be waged up until "the first shovel tears a hole in the heart of Pine Hollow."

My friends and I were deeply confused. Somebody somewhere had to know about all these men and this humungous machinery, right? Bettina and I (two medium-size kids) had been spotted within *one minute* of entering the Bluffs club. Surely a park ranger had noticed an eight-story mining shovel, right? What about the big white canvas tent, the semitrailers, and the Porta-Johns? Had the facts changed? Did Amalgamated Bauxite Industries get a new lease that allowed them to set up a mining camp in Pine Hollow ahead of schedule? None of us thought so. The bauxite mine was the number-one topic of all of our parents and everyone in Surf Island. My friends and I would have been the first to know if the situation had changed.

Din pulled out the bahtphone, but it didn't have any signal this deep into the park. I knew who he had wanted to call—Mr. Mora. He would know the whole story. He would also know what to do if things weren't the way they were supposed to be.

We had to read a Shakespeare play in English class. It was really hard to chop through all the olden-day language, but I remembered this one line from a play about a long-ago king: "Heavy is the head that wears the crown." I remembered that because when I read it, I felt I understood what it meant. I'm not saying I'm the "king" of the Outriders, but for some reason everyone looks to *me* to make decisions. I kind of like it, but it is a huge responsibility. For instance, my friends were looking at me now, wondering exactly what we should do.

I had no idea, but I said, "The Bahtphone doesn't work. That means we're four hours away from being able to report what we've seen. It's noon—why don't we do our climb at the tower, then head back *this afternoon* instead of tomorrow."

This idea was met with great enthusiasm. We could hike up the trail to Eagle Tower and be there in twenty minutes. No reason that we couldn't say good-bye to the spot where the Outriders became the Outriders, right? It all made sense, right? It was a decision we would regret, but we had no way of knowing that at the time. Like that Shakespeare guy said, "Heavy is the head . . ."

EAGLE TOWER REVEALS MORE SECRETS

Normally the trek up the last stretch of Sakemwah Trail is peaceful. There are fewer trees and a gentle breeze greets you on the climb. But we could hear the gigantic machines moving around far below us in the valley. There were also strange pneumatic drill noises, which almost sounded like machine gun fire. It would be very easy to be tensed out about what was happening, but once we came to the end of the trail and saw Eagle Tower, it was as if all the distractions of the day simply disappeared.

Like I said, Eagle Tower isn't some architectural masterpiece. It probably would have been better for everyone if it had been. Maybe they wouldn't be able to put a huge open-pit bauxite mine in the middle of a state park if Eagle Tower had been really ornate and beautiful or if it was important in history like the Alamo or something. Like I said, it was a simple tower with a weird doorway thirty-five feet off the ground.

We all put down our day packs and tore into the sandwiches we had brought. Din and Nar were carrying the heaviest load because they had to lug enough food for Howie. Howie eats a lot of food. Bettina shared her turkey and cheese sandwich with Ki, who seemed to like everything but the bread.

Wyatt, the king of gear, "disappeared" his food in like three seconds. He wanted to waste no time getting to his gear check. Wyatt likes to test every single battery, flashlight lamp, and medical supply in his pack, as well as every piece of climbing gear. We used to tease Wyatt about his safety checklists until his fastidious nature had saved us a few times in Willow Key. Now we were glad that Wyatt did the worrying for the rest of us.

There was no question who would be the lead climber. Ty was so super-humanly strong, he could get a fingerhold or toehold on almost any surface. He also could wedge protection anchors into tight spots, and if they could hold Ty's weight, the rest of us would be more than safe. In about four minutes, Ty was rigging a belay (sort of a rope and pulley deal) at the flat stone roof of the tower. For the rest of us, the climb would be easy. We wouldn't be lead climbing, but top climbing. We would have a rope connected to our harness and if we slipped (not likely) the rope would prevent us from falling. Also, with a top climb, it would be very easy to rappel down the inside of the tower and climb back out. The bottom line is, Ty did all the hard work and the rest of us could just enjoy ourselves.

Nar issued the "stay" command to Howie. Obviously there was no way to bring Howie on the climb with us. I know this because it was discussed. Din and Nar spent a very long time locked in a conversation with Wyatt about rigging some type of mastiff harness. But finally it was decided that Howie would enjoy his day more if he just stayed put. Howie is very, very good at the staying-put aspect of being a dog. If Nar gave the stay command, Howie would wait for the next ice age in the same spot until Nar came back. So Howie got comfortable right up against the base of the tower, and the rest of us made our climb.

I wish I could dazzle you with the danger and complexity of the climb, but we were all standing on the stone roof of the tower in about five minutes. Now you have to take into account that I haven't been many places in the world, but the view from Eagle Tower was world-class AWESOME. I'm not sure it would compare to Machu Picchu in Peru, but people from the Flats don't get to Peru as often as you would think. So for my friends and me it was the most beautiful place on earth. There was a dense swath of deep green pines and far off on the horizon, the blue wisp of Surf Island Lagoon. Every time we made it to the top of Eagle Tower we felt we had accomplished something important, something we would remember for the rest of our lives.

But it was hard to ignore the mining camp. It was like an open sore at the base of the mountain. Since we didn't want to destroy our last trip to our favorite spot, we decided to ignore the rhythmic pulse of the jackhammers and rappel into the tower. Again, Ty would be our leader. As soon as he got to the bottom, he would be holding the belay line and making sure the rest of us were safe.

Bettina once joked that if Ty were a dog he would be a sheepdog—silently watching over and protecting a flock. Bettina was right (of course), but the funny thing was, the one person Ty watched over more than anyone else was *Bettina*. Bettina was kind to Ty on the first day he arrived from Eastern Europe, so now she had her own personal "sheepdog" for life. But Ty watches over the rest of us, as well, and that's another reason he was always first up or down a rope—he insisted on it.

The only tricky part about the rappel down the inside of the tower is getting from the roof to the rectangular doorway just below. It requires a mini-rappel to the doorway, then the lead climber (Ty) has to install a second belay rig on the lower sill of the opening, otherwise the ropes could rub against the stone and possibly sever.

Ty turned his back to the edge and nimbly hopped down five feet to the tower's entrance. As he was about to install the belay rig, we heard him say, "Is broken."

Wyatt was deeply confused. "I checked that belay rig—it's perfect," he called to Ty.

"Stone is broken. Cam is looking now."

In one quick motion Ty was back on the roof. He clipped my harness to the belay rope and said, "Is important."

Here is what I appreciate about my friend Ty: If he says something is important, you could count on the fact that it was important.

I turned my back to the edge and rappelled down to the mysterious thirty-five-feet-high doorway. I saw immediately what Ty had: A four inch square of stone had fallen away on the lower rim of the entrance; picture a seven-year-old who has lost a lower tooth right in the front of his mouth. But that wasn't the "important" thing that Ty was speaking about. The thing I was now staring at changed everything about this expedition and I was certain would change everything about the lives of the Outriders.

The four-inch square of stone that had fallen away exposed something underneath. Carved into the light-colored rock was the image of an eagle, wings outstretched, soaring above Sakemwah Hill. The tips of the eagle's wings were bent gracefully upward and balancing between them was the fiery orb of the sun. Right next to the stone carving was a perfectly round hole, about the circumference of a silver dollar and about an inch deep. The reason Ty knew this carving was important is because he had *seen it before*. So had all the Outriders. It was exactly the same image that was engraved on Mr. Thorpe's *Golden Sextant*. And even more amazing, on the bottom of the Golden Sextant there was a one-inch-long stem that was the circumference of a silver dollar!

My brain had trouble trying to pull my thoughts together. But one thing was clear: The Golden Sextant had something to do with Eagle Tower; in fact I think it was supposed to be fitted into this exact spot! Oh, I just realized, I should quickly fill you in on some stuff you need to know:

SHORT BURST OF HISTORY

Remember Commodore Sternmetz, the guy who our marina is named for? Okay, he was originally thought to be the owner of the Golden Sextant. But Mr. Thorpe found out that the sextant had actually belonged to the pirate El Trueno (which means "the thunder" in Spanish; El Trueno was famous for launching a barrel of gunpowder high in the air to create "thunder" in order to intimidate ships he intended to board). The notorious pirate stole away the heart of Dona Juliana. That is very important because Commodore Sternmetz was also in love with Dona Juliana. So Sternmetz vowed to catch El

Trueno even if it took him the rest of his life.

Meanwhile, in order to escape, El Trueno betrayed Dona Juliana and stole her fortune. It is rumored he HID what was left of the treasure somewhere in the New World, and specifically NEAR SURF ISLAND. We helped Mr. Thorpe uncover some clues about the location of the supposed treasure. It seemed that El Trueno left a complicated jigsaw puzzle of clues. But (AND HERE IS THE IMPORTANT PART), until this moment the Golden Sextant seemed UNCONNECTED with ANYTHING. But this discovery at Eagle Tower meant that the Golden Sextant is a PIECE OF THE PUZZLE! I didn't know then what this puzzle piece actually meant or if it would lead anywhere, but one thing was for certain: Mr. Thorpe needed to hear about it!

Every Outrider needed to see the carving in the stone (even Ki, the newest Outrider), then we all rappelled down the interior of Eagle Tower. There is nothing much happening inside; there are a few ancient wooden beams that look like they could have been part of a floor or stairway. Otherwise the floor is a solid stone slab. We were excited to have completed our expedition, but we couldn't help but speculate about the meaning of the carving. It was Nar who first realized something important.

"That's why this place is called Eagle Tower!"

I can't believe I hadn't made that connection. Remember I told you that no one knew how the tower got its name? Well, whoever made the eagle carving in the stone must have named the tower. Was this place built by Alvaro Bautista di Salamanca, otherwise known as the pirate El Trueno? Was the treasure (if it exists) hidden here, or is the tower only a part of his elaborate set of clues? We were debating every angle of the mystery in the cool, dark interior of the structure, the inside of the tower looking really cool lit only by our flashlights, when we heard Howie BARKING.

Howie is not only a big dog, he is a confident dog. Howie doesn't bark when he wants food. He doesn't bark to get attention. He doesn't bark at other dogs. Howie will only bark when something is vitally *important*.

It would be impossible for me to describe how fast Nar climbed back up to the tower opening and rappelled down the other side. If it were a movie, you would have just seen a puff of smoke where Nar used to be. One by one the rest of us hurried up the ascent of the interior wall and then zipped down the exterior of the tower to the base. I was the second to last. When I rappelled to the bottom I expected to find:

1. Another bear
2. More massive earth-moving vehicles
3. A park ranger kicking us out of the Hollow (we really weren't supposed to climb and enter Eagle Tower)

Here's what I didn't expect to find:

1. A big hole

For some reason Howie dug an enormous hole right at the base of Eagle Tower. Howie's front paws must weigh eighty pounds apiece, so he can really move some dirt.

"That's why Howie was barking? To show us this *hole*?" Shelby said.

I saw Nar's muscles coil. If he feels that his dog has been insulted in any way, he will attack and keep on attacking. It doesn't matter that one of his best friends made the comment.

"Nar, what Shelby *meant* to say is that usually Howie only barks if something is, you know, *crucial*." I had to diffuse the Nar bomb many times per week.

But this time it didn't work.

"Look in the hole, Cam! Look in the hole! You look in there and tell me if Howie wasted your time!" Nar was really worked up. Howie's integrity was at stake and he was not backing down.

So I got on my knees and looked in the hole.

Shelby must have seen my expression, because she got on her knees beside me.

"Oh. My. God," was all she could say.

Everyone else crouched down and looked.

What we saw was a door. It was easy to see the door was from olden times because of the rusty wrought-iron hinges. The door was actually set into the wall of Eagle Tower, but BELOW the level of the interior floor. Picture one of those exterior basement doors that some older houses have. Part of the door had rotted away and because the sunlight was angling into Howie's hole we could see clearly what was behind the door: a steep set of stairs and a tunnel beyond it. Howie had unearthed a portal to a secret basement or chamber.

I looked over at Shelby. Shelby tapped Nar on the shoulder.

"I'm sorry. Howie is amazing. The most incredible dog in the world," Shelby said.

"And don't forget it," Nar said.

At that moment we heard an engine noise above us. I looked up in the sky to see what looked like two guys riding motor scooters with big hang gliding wings. I was confused.

"Wyatt, what are those things?"

"Ultra-lights."

We all had to wait a beat for Wyatt to continue. He loved having all the information.

"Ultra-light aircraft. Actually those two models are called micro-lights. The whole airplane only weighs two hundred and fifty pounds."

"What do you think they're doing here?" Bettina said.

"We should ask them. They're landing," Shelby said.

"Must to be careful," Ty said, never taking his eyes off the two pilots landing the aircraft.

"Why, Ty?" Without realizing it, Wyatt had gotten behind Ty as if for protection.

Ty pointed to the tiny ultra-light planes. "If person flies this machine, he not care about life."

Ty was right, of course. But we didn't know how right he was until it was almost too late.

CHAPTER SIX: DESCENDING

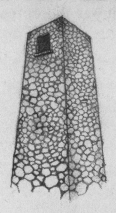

As both pilots climbed out of their ultra-lights, they took off their helmets. I was surprised by two things:

1. They were both sixteen years old.
2. I sort of knew the guys.

The taller one with the thin, angular face was Hunter. His short pudgy friend was Lance. They both lived in the Bluffs. Once or twice a month I would see them at Rocky Point Beach trying to catch some waves. They both had brand-new, top-of-the-line Channel Islands boards and Quiksilver wetsuits. My surf buddies and I call them the "drop-in twins" because they consistently violate the most important rule of surfing and "drop in" when it is not their turn to catch the wave. I'm not sure if you can tell, but I don't like either of them.

"'Sup," Hunter said as he sauntered toward us. Either he didn't recognize me from the beach, or he wanted to pretend he didn't.

"How's it goin', Hunter," I said, just to gain the upper hand.

Lance nudged Hunter. "Hey, it's that gremmie from Rocky Point."

I need to explain something. Surfers use a bunch of slang. But only poser surfers use a word like "gremmie." It's just wrong.

"Cool micro-lights. You build them from a kit?" Wyatt always assumed people were nice, particularly people with cool gear.

Hunter and Lance kind of smirked. They gave the impression that it would be too much effort to answer Wyatt.

In a strange way, I was glad they just insulted my friend. Now the other Outriders knew exactly what we were dealing with.

"Nice lids." Hunter said, and then he and Lance

started chuckling at the rock climbing hats Olivia Ray had given us.

"You guys get *lost* or something?" Shelby said with a slight edge to her voice.

"We discovered this tower," Hunter said.

"Been coming here for years. What's in the mondo hole?" Lance bent down to take a look.

"Mondo" is another one of those words real surfers don't use.

"Check it," Lance said as he dropped down into the hole and pushed his way through the ancient door.

Before I knew what was happening, Hunter had picked up two of our flashlights and was following after his pudgy friend.

"Hey!" Wyatt said, and scrambled in the hole behind them, only concerned for his gear.

One time my dad and I were at a stoplight and the guy in the car next to us just flicked a lit cigarette out of his window into someone's rose garden. I remember exactly what my dad said to me. "You see that guy? He thinks the world is his ashtray." That's what I was thinking about Hunter and Lance when Shelby tapped me on the shoulder.

"We better get down there."

"Duh."

We all grabbed our gear, and in a matter of seconds we had pushed past the ultra-old wooden door and were descending the long set of stone stairs toward the dark tunnel below. The walls were solid dark rock (I think it was basalt, but I don't know much about rocks), which looked nothing like the light stone from Eagle Tower. Our footsteps echoed against the hard surfaces and the group of us sounded like a herd of elephants.

I could see the faint glow of Hunter's and Lance's—that is, OUR—flashlights ahead of us. We let Howie lead the way—not because we were afraid, but because you don't want a 243-pound dog BEHIND you on very steep, slippery steps. Bettina was next to me and I could hear Ki purring in her day pack. The cat might have been relaxed but I was amped up. If Hunter and Lance hadn't flown into our lives, I would have been stoked to explore this secret passage. But the two older guys brought a kind of dark energy into the mix.

Up ahead, I heard Hunter cry out, "WHOA, DUDE! LOOK AT THAT!"

Then Lance yelled, "COWABUNGA!"

Note to all of you: Don't ever say that.

Then I heard Wyatt yell back to us, "GUYS, YOU GOTTA SEE THIS!"

The tunnel at the end of the stairs was just wide enough to walk single file. I began to imagine that I heard rapidly moving water. Our flashlights found Hunter, Lance, and Wyatt standing at the end of the tunnel in what seemed to be some kind of bigger chamber or cave. When we finally caught up with them, I could *feel* that the chamber was much bigger than I had imagined. The flashlights' beams just faded into the inky blackness and it was tough to make out what was ahead.

Wyatt has this piece of gear called a *tactical flashlight*. I don't understand why it is so different from the regular kind of flashlight, but it is ultra-powerful. When he pulled it out of his day pack and clicked it on, I caught a glimpse of water moving—some type of subterranean river. Then, when Wyatt started exploring the chamber with the technical flashlight, I realized that my life and my friends' lives had changed forever.

It wasn't simply a chamber. It was an entire American Indian VILLAGE.

"Ni-ice," Shelby said, which is the highest Shelby compliment.

A LOST WORLD

Hunter, Lance, and the rest of us just stood at the mouth of the tunnel in stunned silence. We all used our flashlights to try to take in the size and scope of what was in front of us.

Have you ever seen pictures of American Indian villages (I think they were called pueblos) that were constructed of adobe and the houses were sort of stacked on top of one another like a staircase? I know most of those were way out west in places like New Mexico and Arizona, but the basic design of the structures here was the same. These houses, made of dark stone (not adobe), were terraced on four levels and set against the towering stone walls of the chamber.

It was fairly easy to figure out what the original village looked like. There must have been two huge caves that faced each other separated by a ravine. The river that coursed through the ravine divided the two sides of the village. Somehow, maybe because of an earthquake or something, the two sides of the village collapsed TOWARD each other, creating a huge mound that became Sakemwah Hill. You know those snow dome souvenirs? The ones you shake and little snowflakes sprinkle down? Picture little stone houses facing one another on opposite sides of the dome, and imagine a tiny river running down the center. Now try to think what that snow dome village would look like if it were a hundred feet high. Howie had dug a tunnel hundreds of years into the past.

I was filled with a sense of awe.

"We totally scored! We're going to be rich!" I heard Hunter say.

He and Lance were on their knees picking up something from the floor of the underground chamber.

"Arrowheads! Look at all this pottery junk! We're gonna be famous like that Indiana Jones dude." Lance was stuffing arrowheads into his cargo shorts.

"STOP IT!" Shelby yelled. "We shouldn't take anything! It doesn't belong to us!"

"You're right, gremmie, it belongs to US." Hunter and Lance barely looked up from what they were doing.

Shelby was about to launch into them again when Bettina took her by the arm. "Let's look around. Forget about those jerks."

"Over here!" Din yelled.

Din, Nar, and Howie had found a sort of circular "room" carved into the wall of rock. Their flashlights illuminated a group of ultra-colorful cave paintings (not sure that is the actual technical term). The paintings were really detailed and went completely around the circumference of the circle. Shelby, Bettina, Wyatt, and Ty joined us in the low-ceilinged room. If the circumstances were different, we would have looked like a group of middle school kids at a museum staring at art on the walls.

"It's a story," Din said.

Din is obsessed with two things: electronics and drawing. Since most of the electronic gear he is interested in costs a bucket of money (which none of us have), he spends most of his time with a pad and pencil creating these elaborate comic books, filled with superheroes, space vehicles, aliens, and a mastiff with artificial intelligence. Din's expertise in the visual arts is the reason we all crowded around him to see what he could decipher from the cave drawings. Now we looked like a group of middle school kids at a museum being taken on a tour by the curator.

"This has to be Mingwa," Din said. He pointed to the figure of a man who was drawn three times larger than any other human figure. In one drawing he was portrayed standing between the two facing caves, his gigantic legs straddling the river. It was as if his body was a bridge between the two halves of the village. Around his neck he wore an amulet of an eagle, wings outstretched, carrying the sun between the tips.

"He had a high opinion of himself," Bettina said.

"He didn't draw these. Some Sakemwah artist did," Din said.

Shelby was looking at a painting of Mingwa, the water chief, standing on a cliff looking out toward the ocean. "So the artist was, like, sucking up to the boss?"

"It's like in a Tom Cruise movie. Whoever makes those has Tom Cruise do all the cool stuff, because he's the star," I said, just to participate.

"That's pretty much the idea," Din said. "Your eye goes to the thing that is most important."

Ty had drifted to the farthest point from the opening of the room and had his flashlight focused on a particular painting. He said, "Is boat. We know."

The group shifted around Ty. All of us raised our flashlights to get a better look.

"Oh. My. God." Once again, Shelby said what we were all thinking.

"*L'Esperanza,*" Wyatt said.

We were looking at a picture of a Spanish galleon named the *L'Esperanza*. On the bow was a very distinctive figurehead of a woman with long flowing black hair. Remember the short burst of history earlier? The figurehead was a carving of Dona Juliana, the woman both Commodore Sternmetz and the pirate El Trueno were in love with. Before you think I'm some kind of freakish history expert, you should know that all of the Outriders *had been on that ship*! (Of course it had been forty-five feet underwater at the time.)

"Wait a minute! El Trueno raided the Sakemwah?" Nar said.

"No, look," Din pointed to another painting. Mingwa and El Trueno were sharing a very elaborately carved pipe.

"They were friends?" Bettina squinted as if it would help her understand.

"I think they took him in—hid him," Din said while pointing to one of the last paintings. "And then Sternmetz came looking for him."

We all shifted over to look at a depiction of a British warship. The artist had even shown the British soldiers boarding El Trueno's galleon and taking brown barrels off the ship and loading them onto rowboats.

"Those barrels—was that El Trueno's treasure?" There was a charge in Shelby's voice like we were on the verge of a major discovery.

"Nope. That was his gunpowder," Din said, pointing at the very last painting.

What we saw next was shocking. This painting seemed much less detailed than the rest. It was more of a sketch. But one thing was clear: It showed Sternmetz and his men putting barrels of gunpowder inside the two facing caves of the Indian village.

"Sternmetz blew up the Sakemwah village? Commodore Sternmetz?" Bettina seemed really rattled. We had all grown up thinking Commodore Sternmetz was some kind of hero, mostly because our marina was named after him.

"I think the Sakemwah warned El Trueno and he escaped. Sternmetz must have been angry," Din said.

"So he blew up a whole village?" Bettina could not wrap her mind around it.

"What happened to the Sakemwah?" Nar asked.

Wyatt now spoke. The history of the Sakemwah was his deal. "Most stuff I've read said that they left this area and joined up with another tribe, maybe the Seminoles."

We all pondered the immensity of this discovery and our direct link to a bunch of cool history. I ran my flashlight over all of the paintings from the first to the last.

"It's not only the Sakemwah's story, it's their blog," I said. Some long-ago artist had decided to put down everything that happened to his people. In a much smaller way, that's what I do for the Outriders. This seemed less interesting to the group than it did to me.

"What about El Trueno's treasure? Do you think he gave it to the Sakemwah in exchange for letting him escape?" Nar said to his brother.

"There's nothing in the pictures about it," Din said.

"El Trueno came back," I said.

All eyes swiveled to me.

"Eagle Tower. The Sakemwah didn't build it—El Trueno did."

"How do *you* know?" Shelby didn't like it if I figured out stuff before she did. It didn't happen often.

"If that tower had been built *before* Sternmetz blew up the village, it wouldn't be standing up straight. The tower, the stairs, and the tunnel would have collapsed with the two caves. Also it is built with that light colored stone. This whole village is built with dark stone. I think El Trueno came back and built Eagle Tower as a monument to his friends. That's why he carved the eagle—it was Mingwa's symbol."

"And he carved it to hide a clue to the treasure," Shelby said.

"Could be," I said.

"What treasure?" We all turned to see Hunter and Lance in the opening to the room. The pockets of their cargo pants and jackets were stuffed with artifacts. I had been having such a cool time with my friends I had almost forgotten that these guys were still roaming around.

"You going to answer me?" Hunter said.

"We're just 'gremmies.' What would we know about any treasure?" Shelby said.

"If there's any treasure, it belongs to *us*, you understand?" Hunter's face was pinched with menace.

Something inside me snapped. It doesn't happen often, but when it does, I can't control what I say. "No, I don't think *you* guys understand! This place could *save* Pine Hollow!"

"Are you whack or what, dude?" Lance said.

"Don't you get it? If we tell people about this place—the right people—they'll stop the mine! No one would let Amalgamated Bauxite dig up a lost city!"

Hunter and Lance laughed really hard.

"You Flat trash are so out of your league. You better learn how the world works," Hunter said.

"Yeah, big always wins." As he said this, Lance pulled up his cargo shorts, which had been weighted down by all the stolen artifacts.

"We're gonna keep our eyes on you. You dig up any treasure, now or ever, you'll see us again."

I heard Nar whispering the Thai word *"pajon"* to Howie. It meant attack. Howie sat up but didn't sense any danger, so he just sat still and took it all in with his huge eyes.

Wyatt pointed to the flashlights Hunter and Lance were holding. "Give me back my gear."

"Don't worry, we'll flush your flashlights down our toilets in the Bluffs; you'll eventually get it down where you live."

"Why don't you two just fly away in your little toy airplanes?" Bettina said, her eyes ablaze with fury.

Lance stared at Bettina for a moment. "Viveca Conroy your sister?"

"None of your business." Bettina's fists were clenched.

"Aw, jealous of big sister?" Lance laughed as he said it.

I didn't even get a chance to stick out my arm to stop Ty. Besides being ultra-strong, Ty moves really quickly. Mr. Barnett, our football coach, had been trying to get Ty into shoulder pads for years. But Ty only wanted to hang out with us (plus he didn't really know the rules of football). But Coach Barnett would have been proud of the flying tackle that took down both Hunter and Lance. *Now* Howie started to bark.

A whole lot of bad things could have happened. Ty could have started throwing punches. The rest of us could have jumped in and started a melee. Nar could have let Howie get into the fight. But, fortunately not one bad thing happened—oh, except for a massive explosion of dynamite.

CHAPTER SEVEN: PANICKING

The entire Sakemwah village shook. We heard a rumble, like an avalanche of rocks.

Hunter and Lance rolled away from Ty and scrambled to their feet. Without so much as a word to the rest of us, they began sprinting for the tunnel entrance. My friends and I should have done the exact same thing, but for some reason we felt compelled to have the following discussion:

MOST USELESS CONVERSATION IN HISTORY
Nar: What was THAT?
Ty: Is dynamite.

Wyatt: They're starting to mine?
Shelby: It seems that way, doesn't it?
Din: But they weren't supposed to start for five more days!
Cam: Apparently they started early.

Then we RAN. Our flashlights joggled in the darkness. Ki began to whine in Bettina's backpack. Howie was unaffected. I wish I had his mastiff disposition, because I was FREAKED OUT.

THINGS I SHOULD HAVE REALIZED EARLIER

1. If a mining company breaks the law and sets up camp five days ahead of schedule, it is logical that they would have no problem setting off dynamite whenever they wanted.
2. After seeing humongous earth-moving equipment and a mining camp, try to stay out of underground areas where blasting may occur.
3. Before rushing down a tunnel into a lost city, realize that if there is an emergency, no one on earth will be able to find you.

Number three was a particularly important point because, when we reached the entrance to the tunnel, the tunnel was gone. Hunter and Lance were trying to move rocks and boulders to clear a path. Some of the boulders weighed at least four tons. It wasn't going to happen.

As I expected, Lance was not good under pressure. "We are so totally MUNCHED! Do you hear me? EL MUNCHO!"

"Chill! I gotta think!" Hunter said.

"There's another way out," I said.

Everyone looked at me.

"You know that or are you guessing?" Hunter said.

"The Sakemwah lived in these two caves, right? What if another tribe came to attack? Or what if the river overflowed? They'd have some secret escape route, right?"

"So, you're *guessing*." Hunter almost spat at me as he spoke.

"I'm *hoping*," I said.

There was another thunderous explosion. This time one of the Sakemwah houses on the top level collapsed and fell to the cave floor. Some small rocks rained down. One bonked off Ty's climbing helmet. I said a silent prayer of thanks for Mr. Mora.

The absolute worst thing was my friends looked at me as if I would know what to do. That Shakespeare "heavy is the head" thing ran through my brain again.

"We gotta search every inch of this place. See if there's another way out," I said.

"You think you're the big kahuna? As if!" Lance said.

"Enough of you, gremmie. We're booking." Hunter tapped Lance on the shoulder and they ran into the darkness. We watched their flashlight beams grow dimmer as they got farther away. I was never happier to see two people leave. Now my friends and I could get down to business.

In those Tom Cruise action movies, if, for instance, a group of people are trapped in an underground lost city, somebody will always say, "Let's split up." But in real life, this is an insanely bad idea. It's far better to know where everyone is at all times. That's why we Outriders stayed in a very tight clump and started frantically searching the Sakemwah village for an exit.

We went back into the circular painting room to see if we missed some type of secret panel. We climbed into every one of the houses (except the one that had caved in from the dynamite) looking for trap doors. We walked along the stone walls with

133

our flashlights searching for any trace of an opening. We were all jittery and tense, just waiting for the next explosion.

Occasionally we could hear Hunter and Lance calling to each other. They, of course, had split up.

Another difference between Tom Cruise movies and real life: Tom always, always finds a way out of a tough situation. Sure, there may be a space alien or a paid assassin between him and freedom, but Tom always comes through. And for sure Tom Cruise never has the following conversation:

SECOND MOST USELESS CONVERSATION IN HISTORY
Nar: What time is it?
Bettina: What difference does it make?
Nar: I have to feed Howie.
Shelby: We've got bigger problems, Nar.
Nar: He gets really hungry.
Wyatt: We're trapped underground, Nar.
Nar: Howie doesn't know that.
Cam: Nar, we need to focus on the *dynamite*.
Nar: Why can't we focus on Howie?

So that's when Ty grabbed Nar's day pack, ripped it open, took out a handful of kibble, and held it under Howie's muzzle. There was a SCHLURP sound and the food disappeared.

Ty said, "Is fed now."

And the world lurched sideways. The dynamite blast was so strong, a whole level of the Sakemwah village was flattened. We were in a bad spot and it was getting worse every minute.

"We gotta try the other side of the cave!"

I led the group to the edge of the underground river. It was only about twenty feet wide. But it was one of the most dangerous stretches of water I had ever seen.

If there is one thing I know well it is water, especially water that moves. This river looked very placid on the surface. But I knew the current would be insanely powerful. Any time water is trapped in a confined space and then gets a chance to run free, you will have a powerful current. Surfers know this all too well. Anytime you paddle near a storm drain, you may find yourself swept out to sea as if you'd been caught in a riptide. Down here in the Sakemwah village, the river was flowing from an underground channel and getting a brief chance to run free before it disappeared again into a narrow opening. In effect, this meant that the rocks were acting like a nozzle of a hose, focusing the power of the water.

Wyatt said, "We can swim this, right?" It was less of a question, more of a prayer.

"No way." I dug a pencil out of my day pack and tossed it into the middle of the river. The second the pencil hit the surface it got swept toward the narrow opening and was sucked inside like a fly going into a frog's mouth.

"What do we do?" Shelby is brave, but her toughness was fraying at the edges.

I took off my sweatshirt and shoes.

"You're not going in there," Bettina said.

I clipped a carabiner to my climbing belt and hooked the static line to it. Ty understood what I was doing. He went as far upstream as he could and anchored a bunch of chocks into seams in the rock. He then clipped himself to the rope as extra protection.

"Cam, you can't—"

And I was in the water. I'm used to the shock of cold when you dive into the ocean. But most of the time, when I'm surfing, I have my wet suit. I learned something new: underground water is Antarctic cold. And it took me like it took the pencil.

I was swept straight toward the narrow opening. If the line didn't hold, I would be smashed inside of it, and there would be no chance of escape. But the line held. Water rushed over my head. It was as if I was a boulder in the middle of a rapid. But I knew that I just had to relax and angle my body like a surf fin or a surfboard skag and let the current do all the work. In a few seconds I had swung to the opposite bank. The most difficult part of the whole operation was getting a grip on the slippery rock and pulling myself out of the torrent.

When I finally stood up on the other side, my friends actually cheered. Wyatt handed Ty a day pack full of rock anchors. Ty tossed the pack to me and we both went to work. Ty found a tall boulder and anchored a belay rig. I found a good spot very low on a wall to anchor on my side. We had set up a rudimentary zip line. It would be easy for the Outriders to get up on the boulder and swoosh across the river landing safely on this side. As I was securing the last bolt, a thought hit me.

"Howie," I said to myself.

As I turned back toward my friends, I saw Wyatt

and Nar working on linking two climbing harnesses together and putting them around Howie's massive shoulders.

I yelled across to them, "We can't put him on the belay line! He'd hurt himself."

"We're not going to leave him!" Nar said.

"Of course not! But he's going to have to swim!" I yelled.

"He'll get sucked down that hole!" Nar said.

"Not on my watch!" I said with more bravado than real confidence.

There was another explosion. This time the shockwaves knocked us all down. I now had a ringing in my ears.

There was no more time to think. One by one, Shelby (with Ki), Bettina, Wyatt, and Din came across the belay cable. Ty connected a static line to Howie's climbing harness. He anchored the other end of the rope to a rock wall. Then he connected a SECOND line to Howie's harness and held on to the free end as he zipped across the river. Howie now had two layers of protection—that is, if his climbing harness held. Howie endured all this activity in his usual manner—very calmly. He had no idea what was in store for him.

It was going to be Nar's responsibility to get Howie into the river. If this had been another time and place, we all would have found the two climbing harnesses straddling Howie's massive chest comical. Howie just stared at the water. All animals have a deep instinct for self-preservation. Even a dog that loved the water, like a Labrador retriever, would never have thought to put his paws into this icy torrent. Nar tried every Thai command he could think of. Howie remained unmoved. Nar couldn't bring himself to just PUSH Howie into the water. He didn't have the stomach for it. Finally the dynamite blast made it easier. The ground shook and Howie FELL into the river.

All of us were manning the line. But a 243-pound mastiff is not very aqua dynamic. The water pushed hard against the dog. The worst possible thing was happening: Howie was being pushed DOWN under the raging column of water. Ty got up on a boulder so that the line would pull Howie more to the surface. I saw Howie working his powerful paws. I pulled the static line more toward the bank to angle Howie much as I had done. In an instant Howie swung to our bank, but he couldn't find any way to lift himself out of the water. His massive paws struggled to find traction on the slippery rocks.

We worked as a group. While keeping the rope taught, we all went hand over hand to move closer to Howie. The moment we were close Ty and I reached to grab his climbing harness and collar. All the other Outriders grabbed on to us and YANKED. Howie's front paws lifted onto shore, and with one powerful pump he lifted his rear legs onto land.

I realized I hadn't taken one breath during the whole struggle. It looked as if everyone else had been just as tense. Howie then rewarded us by shaking himself dry; the spray doused everyone with buckets of water. By this time Nar had zipped across the belay line and was hugging and kissing his dog. Howie licked Nar, his tongue almost as wide as his master's face.

Our joy was short-lived as we realized we were still trapped in an underground lost city with no way to escape. Shelby had brought over my sneakers and my sweatshirt, but I was frozen to the bone. For some reason, Wyatt had packed an extra T-shirt, so I slipped it on even though it was two sizes too small. The shirt read GOOGLE ME—I'M FAMOUS! We gathered up the ropes and the gear. My teeth were chattering but I felt like we really accomplished something. But would it be enough?

THE OTHER SIDE

We repeated our search procedure on the opposite side of the village. The rear walls of the former cave had lots of nooks and crannies, but all were dead ends. We couldn't find anything in the terraced houses. Near a huge round stone structure—it looked like it held water at one time (Wyatt said it was called a cistern)—we found a room carved into the rock. At first we thought it was another "gallery" of paintings. But it turned out to be full of clay pottery. A lot of the pots were perfectly intact. They were beautiful and ornate. One huge clay pot (maybe it was a water jug or an urn; I'm not a big pottery guy) was an image of Mingwa's head. The mouth, nose, and eyes were sort of sculpted on one side of the pot, and the rounded handles that jut out from the side were shaped like ears. Because of how the lip of the pot was shaped, it looked like Mingwa had really short black hair.

Maybe that's why Shelby said to Bettina, "It looks like your dad gave Mingwa a buzz cut." Shelby took hold of one of the jug handles and said, "Just raise your hand if I lop off one of your ears." That's what Mr. Conroy always says to any kid who sits down in his barber chair.

Shelby was probably trying to lighten the mood by pointing out a funny detail about the Mingwa pottery. I didn't think much of it; I was too busy searching for an exit so we wouldn't be trapped in the underground village forever. But I felt Ty tap me on the shoulder.

He pointed to Bettina. The beam of my flashlight glinted off tears streaming down her face. Shelby saw the same thing I did, and was immediately at her best friend's side.

"What's the matter?" Shelby said.

"My dad." Bettina looked down

"I was just making a stupid joke about the pot," Shelby said.

"Not that." Bettina's tears now plopped onto the stone floor.

See, I was having that problem understanding what goes on inside of girls' heads. I understood we were in a tight situation, but Bettina is awesome under pressure. What was going on?

"What's up with your dad?" Which is what I should have said, but Shelby said it first.

The rest of us crowded around, wanting to support Bettina. There was a long pause as Bettina tried to pull herself together.

"What's the matter? Is your dad sick?" Din said.

"No."

We all waited. I tried to remember if I'd ever seen Bettina cry before. I couldn't remember a time.

"He's leaving." More tears flowed from the corners of Bettina's eyes.

"Leaving your mom?" Wyatt looked shocked. We had all known the Conroys since we'd been born. It didn't add up.

"His reserve unit has been called up. He's going to war," Bettina said.

Shelby hugged Bettina as the rest of us contemplated the enormity of this. Mr. Conroy runs the Cut Hut with Bettina's mom. He is a really nice man who does all the men's and children's cuts. Two times a year he smokes a cigar—his private way of celebrating the birth of his two daughters. While Mrs. Conroy calls herself a "hair stylist," Mr. Conroy calls himself a "barber." When you own a small business, health insurance is really expensive. So ten years ago, Mr. Conroy joined the Army Reserves so he could take care of his family.

I know all this because Turner Conroy is my dad's best friend. It was hard to imagine that the U.S. Army needed a forty-year-old barber to fight their battles for them. Sometimes the world is less than fair.

"Now we're stuck down here. I won't get a chance to say good-bye." Bettina tried to dry her tears with the sleeve of her shirt.

"*Naj te ne skrbi*," Ty said. When Ty was *really* serious, he said stuff in his native language. Just a few months back we all discovered that Ty had lost his mother during a war in his home country. He carried around the only existing picture of his mom in his wallet. Ty is a tough guy to read, but I knew for sure he didn't want Bettina to ever have to go through what he did. So obviously I had no idea what the words he had said meant, but I knew he was telling Bettina not to worry.

"We're going to get out of here, Bettina," I said.

"You know that or are you guessing?" she said with a small smile.

"I'm hoping." I smiled back.

"We've gotta search every corner of this place!" Shelby said really loudly.

I think she was trying to be strong for Bettina.

We all started feeling around the rocks for any kind of opening.

I know I should have been totally focused on escaping, but my thoughts drifted. Sometimes, when I am alone out in the surf or off by myself paddling a kayak, strange thoughts pop into my head. Now I was on my hands and knees looking for some passageway through the rock walls and those same strange thoughts crept up on me. I was thinking about my mom. She split when I was really young; my dad and Kyle refuse to say a word about her. They don't actually *refuse*; they just change the subject or find something they have to do. That makes me feel even more alone, because I have so many questions about her and no one to ask.

QUESTIONS ABOUT MY MOM

1. What was she like?
2. Why did she leave?
3. Does she miss me and Kyle?
4. Why won't anyone talk about her?
5. Will I ever see her again?

I guess the whole thing with Bettina and her dad going to war made me dwell on this subject.

Bettina spends a lot of time with her dad, and when he deploys, she is going to miss him and worry about him. She's going to think about those two cigars he smokes every year and the way he always says, "Raise your hand if I lop off one of your ears." But when I think about my mom, I don't have any of those memories. It's like an empty space on the wall where a picture used to be. You feel like something should be there, but it's not. It seemed kind of selfish to be thinking about this stuff, but that's the way it is with strange thoughts—they just come into your head whenever they want to.

"I can't find anything," Shelby said. "Let's look somewhere else."

Just as we were about to exit the room, Ki started to screech, almost as if she was fighting with another cat in Bettina's day pack.

Bettina had reached in to get Ki to comfort her, but the cat went berserk and leaped out of Bettina's arms and ran underneath a stone overhang. Our flashlights whipped over to look for Ki. Out of the corner of my eye I saw a blur, and I naturally assumed it was the cat. But all of a sudden, Ki POUNCED on the spot where I had seen the blur.

We were fighting for our very survival and Bettina's new pet had decided to chase a mouse. You see what I mean about cats?

"Ki, forget the mouse. Come here, pretty girl, "Bettina said.

Then it hit me. A mouse!

"How did a mouse get down here?" I asked the group.

We found it right above the overhang. It was a narrow opening, maybe four feet wide. And it was man-made. It almost looked like a "vent" that the Sakemwah installed for this pottery room. Wyatt lit a match and we watched as the smoke floated upward, drawn by a current of AIR.

Ki must have lost track of the mouse, because she started purring and rubbing up against Bettina's legs. Bettina scooped up the ocicat and kissed her.

"You're a lousy hunter, but a very brave girl," Bettina said.

Wyatt was already in the vent. He was small and wiry and was able to shimmy at an amazingly rapid rate. There was a curve in the vent and Wyatt disappeared. We all waited for what seemed like an eternity.

"I SEE THE SUN!" Wyatt screamed.

"HELP!" someone screamed, but it wasn't Wyatt. The scream had come from the direction of the river.

"It's those two boneheads," Shelby said.

I looked at Ty and sighed. He nodded.

"Shelby, you Bettina, Din, and Nar try to get Howie up through that vent."

"If you're staying down here, I'm staying down." Shelby hated to miss any type of action, even if it meant she was in danger.

"No time to argue," I said as Ty and I sprinted back toward the river.

COWABUNGA

As I ran, I pulled the rock-climbing rope out of my day pack. I knew what was going on near the river, even if it was too dark to see. One of the boneheads had tried to swim across. I just hoped he was still around when we got to him.

He was, but barely. It was Hunter who had tried to make the crossing. I can't believe that anyone who has ever gone out into the ocean on a surfboard could have made a mistake of this magnitude.

I have to give Lance credit. He had tried to save

his friend and gotten himself into one of the most painful positions imaginable. Lance was lying flat on his back. One leg was dangling out into the water. His friend Hunter had a death grip on it. The other leg was straddling a large rock near the edge of the rushing river. The current was pulling HARD against Hunter, and that meant that Lance's legs were being pulled apart like a wishbone. We had a few seconds before something tragic happened.

I pulled off my climbing harness, clipped it to the line, then tossed that whole rig over the river to Lance. Lance caught it and reached down to hand it to Hunter. Ty had already started anchoring the line.

The most dangerous moment was when Hunter let go with one hand to grab the harness. All he could manage to do was stick his arm into one of the leg holes and loop it around. At that moment the current ripped him off of Lance's leg and he went shooting straight for the narrow opening.

Ty and I grabbed the line and leaned all of our weight in the opposite direction of the flow. Hunter actually disappeared into the narrow opening for a moment, and I thought for sure it was as bad as it could get. But Ty pulled with all his might, and suddenly Hunter's head bobbed above the water and we managed to guide him to the far bank. We were now experienced in the hand-over-hand line shimmy, and we made our way to Hunter and pulled him out.

He had taken in so much water, he had a coughing jag for a few minutes. In the meantime Ty had tossed the line across and Lance was able to belay much as we had earlier.

Lance ran over to his friend. "What a rad cruncher, dude!"

Because sometimes the universe gets it right, Hunter threw up all over Lance.

Another EXPLOSION brought us all back to our senses.

"We found a way out."

"Where?" Lance said.

Ty pointed toward the pottery room.

Hunter could have said:

1. "Thank you both for saving my life."
2. "That was brave of both of you."
3. "You two are awesome for finding a way to escape."

Instead he and Lance ran toward the air vent without saying a word.

By the time we reached the vent, everyone had shimmied to the surface. I motioned to Ty. He was reluctant to go ahead of me.

"You're bigger. You may get stuck. If you do, I'll push," I said.

Ty smiled, which he doesn't often do, and climbed into the vent. I got in behind him. Ty is so powerful that he made much better time than I did. When I finally saw the bright sliver of sunlight near the surface, I thought I would shout for joy. But for some reason Ty stopped short at the mouth of the vent. He then did the strangest thing: He KICKED ME BACK farther into the vent.

I heard him say, "What you wanting?"

Ty then tapped his foot twice against the tunnel and exited. I had no idea what that foot tap meant, but I knew it was a signal. Ty didn't want me to come to the surface, only I couldn't figure out why.

I heard voices. But they weren't voices I recognized. Ty wouldn't have warned me unless something big was happening. It took all of my willpower not to stick my head out and look at what was happening.

But if for some reason Ty thought it was important for me not to be seen, then I would do as he said. At least for a few minutes.

BACK TO THE SURFACE

I could only last five. Very carefully I shimmied my way to the surface. Then I slowly lifted my head through the opening and immediately understood why Ty had warned me: A semicircle of miners had surrounded the Outriders, Hunter, and Lance. My friends were backed up against the lowered mining shovel of the BEHEMOTH we had seen earlier. The steel face of the shovel looked like the jaws of a thousand-ton shark.

One of the miners called to the foreman, "What do you want to do with 'em, Mr. Trasker?"

Trasker, the foreman, was wide; he had a big gut that hung over his belt. He had mutton-chop side-burns and wore one of those biker wallets with a chain connected to the belt loop on his work pants. The back of his shirt said ABI in big letters. All the miners wore yellow hard hats with the same logo.

"Y'know, an open pit mine is just about the most dangerous place you can be snooping around. Lots of accidents happen. Lots of people go missing. . . ."

So, clearly that was a *threat*. Trasker wasn't concerned that he almost blew up a bunch of kids with dynamite. This was bad, very bad. I couldn't put it all together in my head, but it meant that Amalgamated Bauxite Industries must have been doing something REALLY, REALLY WRONG and they were really angry that we found out. I felt like we had been safer trapped in the underground city.

I saw Ty glance briefly in my direction. He gave an almost imperceptible nod. Like I said, one of the great things about having best friends is you know what they are thinking. Remember when Bettina, Wyatt, and I were up at the Bluffs Country Club? Wyatt knew Bettina and I were going to be chased and he just disappeared down the Escape Trail. That is because all of the Outriders know:

1. There is no reason for everyone to be caught.
2. If the others are in trouble, go get help.

So it was up to me.

I knew exactly what Ty would do next. He

wanted to give me a chance to escape unseen, so he was going to create a distraction. Distractions are what the Outriders do best. So I peered over the rim of the vent hole as Ty threw a coil of mountain-climbing rope right at the foreman, Trasker. A lot happened fast. Two miners started to make a move for Ty. Immediately Howie started growling. The miners wanted no part of Howie. I saw Trasker signal with his hand. In one lighting-fast SCOOP, the ginormous shovel dug into the dirt and RIPPED THE GROUND out from under my friends. I watched them slide into the maw of the shovel as it tilted upward. They were now trapped in the world's largest steel bowl. The operator lifted the shovel high in the air. Even if one of my friends could climb to the edge of the trap, they would be dangling forty feet above the ground.

By this time I was sprinting across the Table. Our whole underground journey had taken us only about eight hundred yards from Eagle Tower. I sprinted toward it. I thought I could make it there undetected, but I heard a SIREN sounding. A pickup truck started zooming toward me.

My plan had been to hike out of the Hollow,

maybe even find a ranger along the way. But now I was minutes away from being caught.

Obviously I was never going to be able to outrun them—they had a truck.

But I had a plane—even if it was a small one.

CHAPTER EIGHT: SOLOING

I would have never been able to get off the ground if it wasn't for a foreign film called *Tears and Whispers*.

I should explain. When my brother Kyle was still in high school, he kind of slacked off in the homework and chore departments (this should come as no big surprise). My father sought to correct this by mandating that Kyle earn chore credits by looking after his little brother (me). Kyle accepted this deal willingly, because he knew that "looking after" me meant taking me to the movies, where he could meet his friends or, more important, pursue whichever girl he was interested in at the time.

For a brief three week period Kyle chased very hard after Jenny Andrews. Jenny was really beautiful and was the only girl in Surf Island who wore a strand of pearls and her hair in a French braid (this was explained to me in detail by Shelby). Jenny was also deeply interested in all things French (not just her braid) and wanted to see a film called *Larmes á Voix Basse* (*Tears and Whispers*). Under normal circumstances Kyle would have preferred jumping into a tree shredder to seeing a French subtitled film with no digital effects, but for Jenny he was willing to make any sacrifice. Since I was being dragged to the movie and Kyle didn't want me sitting anywhere near him or Jenny Andrews (and her French perfume), I was required to wait in the lobby, where the only thing of any entertainment value was an arcade video game called FireFlight.

FireFlight is one of those flight simulator games where you operate the controls and the cockpit actually moves to make you feel like you are flying. I'm not a big video-game guy (I never caught the SporeSlayer virus), but FireFlight was pretty cool. The whole point of the game was to take off from an aircraft carrier in an F-18 Joint Strike Fighter, shoot down a whole bunch of enemy targets, and then land back on the carrier before your fuel ran out. Since *Tears and Whispers* was a really, really long movie and Kyle had loaded me up with a few rolls of quarters, I got pretty good at completing my missions. I had no way of knowing at the time that the long, dull French movie would save my life.

When I hopped into the ultra-light plane, the first thing I noticed was that none of the buttons or controls looked anything like FireFlight. The arcade video game was very colorful and full of digital dials and lights. The ultra-light had a few buttons and a small green analog display with three dials. It was actually very disappointing from a design standpoint. But there was a switch clearly labeled "IGNITION."

I could hear the pickup truck zooming toward Eagle Tower as the propeller of the ultra-light started spinning. The one clearly identifiable airplane control was the stick. There was a thing that looked like a bicycle brake attached to it which I guessed was the throttle. So, not knowing what else to do, I squeezed it to the maximum, the engine RACED, and the plane started moving forward!

The driver of the Amalgamated Bauxite Industries pickup started beeping his horn. Perhaps he hoped to make me rethink my attempt to escape and consider surrendering. As if.

I was amazed at how responsive the small plane was. As the ultra-light started to accelerate, I could feel the wings wanting to lift it off the ground. This was a very fortunate thing as *I had completely run out of mesa*. In my desire to get away from the pickup, I had neglected to keep track of my position on the Table and my plane was just about to fall off the edge of the cliff! So I did exactly what I learned playing FireFlight and pulled back on the stick.

I guess I was really tensed out because I pulled back *way too hard*. I almost accomplished my first takeoff and first loop-de-loop at the same moment. Also I discovered something I did not learn in the FireFlight simulator game: Planes tend to *stall* when they fly straight up. Oh, and when they stall, they *fall*. So I actually almost accomplished a first in aviation history: a takeoff, loop-de-loop, stall, fall, and crash.

What saved me is the buoyancy (I don't know if that is an airplane term) of the ultra-light. It seemed to "float" downward, and in that moment the engine stormed back to life and I found myself airborne. I was actually flying an airplane!

Since I hadn't been paying any attention to direction or altitude (just trying to save my life) I realized I was now flying AWAY from Surf Island and BACK toward the mining camp. I also discovered I was headed directly toward the pickup truck. The driver of the truck looked stunned that I was actually zooming back in his direction. Or maybe he was shocked that I was only *four feet off the ground*. It might have also appeared that I was TAUNTING him as I was wiggle-waggling the wings of the airplane trying to find out how the controls worked. Even though I was frantic to gain altitude, I pulled back more gently on the stick. This technique worked like a charm and I angled upward in a graceful climb. The ABI pickup sped underneath me as I lofted into the wild blue yonder.

Another problem: I couldn't really figure out how to TURN. The stick seemed to TILT the plane and not turn it. Near my feet I saw some PEDALS. I put my sneakers on them and pushed. I made EXACTLY the same mistake as I had with the stick: I did it much too hard, and the ultra-light made a furious banking turn that shook the wings and strained the engine. But somehow, miraculously, I was now headed toward Surf Island. I vowed to treat the controls more sensitively and thus prolong my life.

I had been in the freezing water of the underground river. My jeans were still sopping wet. Wyatt's two-sizes-too-small T-shirt provided no warmth. My teeth were chattering from the cold or it might have been because my friends were in danger and I was afraid.

I looked down at the small green analog panel. One of the dials was marked "ALT," which I assumed was my altitude. I was currently flying at 150 feet. I had no idea whether or not that was too high or too low. There was another dial that showed a diagram of a little airplane and when I tilted my wings, the little airplane on the dial did the same. I assumed that dial was supposed to help me keep the ultra-light level with the horizon, but it was trickier than it might seem. There was also a fuel gauge and I was happy to see that I wasn't in danger of running low on gas; it was more than half full.

Surfing is awesome, riding on top of Galloway was a rush, but I have to admit, it is possible that flying an ultra-light tops them all. Sure, I was freezing cold and had no idea what I was doing, but the RUSH of freedom and the awesome view was totally worth it. I had now climbed to about two hundred feet in the air above Sakemwah Trail. The Hollow looked incredible from above. The mid-afternoon sun was off to my right. The pine forest looked more like rolling hills of deep green. I could see a herd of deer bounding through a meadow. I could see Titan Grove, where some of the oldest and tallest pines on earth grew. I have never been to a redwood forest, but I couldn't imagine trees any taller than the Titans. Off in the distance I could see the foamy green and bright aqua waters of Surf Island Lagoon and, beyond it, my hometown. I had made the mistake of enjoying myself for a few minutes. That's probably why I didn't hear the helicopter.

There must be a lot of bauxite under Sakemwah Hill. All that bauxite must be worth a bucketful of money. Why else would an ABI helicopter be zooming toward me? You have to have a lot at stake if you are trying to ram a middle school kid in an ultralight and knock him out of the sky.

I had only been a pilot for twenty minutes, but that was enough to know that I was in deep trouble. The helicopter was faster, more powerful, and more maneuverable. I tried to think of a category in which the ultra-light bested the helicopter but could come up with exactly one: My plane was much *lighter*. But I couldn't figure out a way to use that to my advantage. I looked down and could see our scavenged Old Town Trippers tucked into Shady Cove. The joyous canoe crossing of Surf Island Lagoon seemed a lifetime ago. And then the plane *dropped*.

Apparently water cools the air. I don't know anything about aerodynamics or lift; I just know that an ultra-light is very sensitive to changes in temperature. An experienced pilot would have anticipated this when crossing from the Hollow out into the lagoon. But it was my inexperience and ineptitude that might have saved me for the moment.

The helicopter pilot, who seemed to me to be really excellent at his job, was hoping to nudge me with one of his skids, or perhaps let his rotor tear up my wing. But he could never have anticipated my sudden drop in altitude. He was just about on my tail when my ultra-light fell toward the water. My shocking maneuver caused this very experienced pilot to OVERCORRECT, and he spun past my position. I was now flying only about thirty feet above the lagoon and trying hard to think of some possible way to avoid being ripped out of the sky by the helicopter.

I could see the side door of the copter OPEN to reveal the foreman, Mr. Trasker, sitting in the passenger seat. He had a small pair of binoculars in his hands and was focusing on me.

I must have been quite the sight, a twelve-year-old guy in an ultra-light wearing a rock-climbing helmet and a too-small GOOGLE ME—I'M FAMOUS! T-shirt. Mr. Trasker motioned to the helicopter pilot. The chopper veered in my direction. Now that the pilot understood my erratic flight behavior, I would not be able to fool him again (even unintentionally).

I now became aware of ONE more advantage the ultra-light has over the helicopter: engine noise. My engine was more of a high-pitched *whirr*, but the helicopter sounded loud and robust. Boaters down in the lagoon were peering up into the sky, wondering what kind of bizarre dogfight was playing itself out in the skies over Surf Island. Maybe one of them would send out a distress signal for me.

I briefly considered bailing out into the water. But I realized that I was traveling more than sixty miles per hour and the fall from the cockpit into the water would not turn out well for me or my internal organs. The helicopter pilot apparently didn't care how many boaters might be watching (showing how desperate the situation had become) and was fast approaching, and I didn't have an inkling of a plan until I saw the familiar roof line of Falcon's Lair.

I realized the sixteenth fairway behind Mr. Thorpe's estate would make an ideal landing site for the ultra-light. It was very wide, almost like a four-lane highway. Also it was FLAT, which made it more like a runway.

THINGS I FORCED MYSELF NOT TO THINK ABOUT

1. I had little confidence I could make it to the golf course before the helicopter would intercept me.
2. If I made it, there would certainly be golfers on the course and they would be in danger.
3. I DID NOT KNOW HOW TO LAND AN ULTRA-LIGHT OR ANY OTHER TYPE OF AIRCRAFT.

Number three was really the one that was a blinking red light in my mind. When I played FireFlight, it took me about fifteen dollars worth of quarters to get good at landing on the aircraft carrier deck. The point being, I crashed a lot before I got the hang of it. In the video game, each fifty cents allows you

165

to reset the game. In real life, I would have ONE SHOT at landing. I would either pull it off or it would be GAME OVER.

The helicopter buzzed me. The backwash from the rotors sent me zigzagging all over the sky. I now DIPPED BELOW the level of the Bluffs. I didn't think I was a good enough pilot to gain the altitude to get over them, so I did one of those EVASIVE MANEUVER turns I had discovered back at Eagle Tower.

I just made it. My wingtips were only a few yards from the edge of the Bluffs. I was now running south, parallel to the cliffs. I realized that the closer I could keep to the vertical wall of the Bluffs, the harder it would be for the helicopter to buzz me or ram me because the span of its blades was much wider than my little dinky plane. I realized my puny size might work as an advantage.

When you are playing defense in basketball, the coach will always tell you that the sideline is like another teammate. If you can angle your man away from mid-court and squeeze him against the side-lines, you have effectively sandwiched him between two defenders. I was doing the same thing with the Bluffs. The helicopter could approach me from the lagoon side but would not dare to get too close to the jutting rocks and trees of the Bluffs. Plus I knew every twist and turn of Surf Island, so advantage: me.

The problem was, I was running out of protective cover. I was about to reach the south end of Surf Island Lagoon. I had an idea, but, to use the basketball analogy, it would require a full-court three-point shot at the buzzer.

THE LAST PLAY

I had no desire to return to Goat's Neck Bridge after the Tube-O-Topia disaster. But the low-lying bridge might be my last chance to shake the helicopter.

As soon as I was fifty yards from the end of the Bluffs, I DOVE toward the lagoon. The helicopter had been waiting for me to get away from the cliffs and dove after me.

I noticed that going DOWN, the ultra-light picked up a lot of speed. This worked to my tactical advantage but made me very nervous. The wings of the plane began to vibrate. More important, the downward speed was going to make it harder for an inexperienced pilot (me) to level off at just the right altitude to GO UNDER THE BRIDGE.

The helicopter pilot must have had some combat experience, because he was diving right on my tail. When I was about fifty feet above the water, I pulled back on the stick and used that little airplane dial to try to get level. I should have eased the throttle, but I was so tensed out, I still had it on full.

I heard the whining roar of the helicopter engine rapidly change course to avoid colliding with the bridge. I WHOOSHED under the roadway and just made it through the trestles!

You might be thinking, "What good did this maneuver do for him? The helicopter will just go OVER the bridge and catch up with him on the other side." *Which is exactly what happened.* But the helicopter pilot didn't know one small fact that I knew: The Cedar Cape Coast Guard Station was just a few hundred yards to the south, and I was headed right for it!

But I didn't make it.

I was only about nine feet off the water and I clipped the radar antenna off a Coast Guard forty-four-foot motor lifeboat. The boat looked insanely familiar.

The sudden jolt to my landing gear caused the plane to angle toward the ocean. I did another patented pull-back on the stick and the nose of the plane went straight UP. Now the engine really stalled, and I fell into the ocean.

The tail of the little plane hit first and then I was flipped BACKWARD. The wings hit next. I hadn't had time to fasten my seatbelts, which turned out to be a good thing, because I popped out of the cockpit like a watermelon seed and splashed into the ocean head first.

You would think I would have freaked out, but I had left one arena I knew NOTHING about and entered one that I knew A LOT about. As shocking as my crash was, I knew that I could kick and find the surface and be a lot better off than if I was up in the air being chased by a mining company helicopter.

As I emerged from the water, I took a deep breath of beautiful Surf Island air. I saw the helicopter receding into the distance.

"YOU AGAIN?" I looked up to see Lieutenant Corkin speaking into a bullhorn.

"I NEED A RESCUE!" I yelled to him.

"I'M NOT SURE I WANT TO!" Lieutenant Corkin was not smiling when he said this.

"ALL MY FRIENDS ARE IN DANGER!" I

screamed. I didn't look like I was joking either.

"YOU ARE PAYING FOR MY RADAR!" he said, and tossed me a life preserver.

Twenty minutes later I was dressed in a blue Coast Guard uniform (way too big). I was also flying in a bright orange Coast Guard Jayhawk helicopter cruising at two thousand feet over the Hollow. There were TWO MORE helicopters on either side of us (possibly the coolest thing ever).

The pilot, Chief Petty Officer Mike Eddy, spoke into an intercom and said, "Lock and load gentlemen."

The helicopters started to descend.

I had left Eagle Tower as a lone aviator and I was now returning with the air cavalry.

Only one problem: The mining equipment, the mining camp, and my best friends were gone.

CHAPTER NINE: SEARCH-AND-RESCUING

I had just spent the past hour telling Lieutenant Corkin everything. I started with the trek to Eagle Tower, our observation of the mining equipment, Howie's discovery of the tunnel, Hunter and Lance's arrival, our descent into the lost city, the explosions of dynamite, the crossing of the underground river, the discovery of the secret exit, and the capture of my friends by the miners and their foreman, Mr. Trasker. It was a mind-blowing story and I could see that Lieutenant Corkin was having a tough time bending his mind around certain aspects.

Keep in mind Lieutenant Corkin only knew me

as a kid who tows humongous truck inner tubes behind a Boston Whaler while being chased by angry water-skiers—I wasn't the most credible guy he'd ever had a conversation with.

My hunch was confirmed about his skepticism when he said, "You rigged a rock-climbing harness to a two-hundred-and-forty-three-pound mastiff to cross an underground river in a lost Indian village?"

"Actually it was two harnesses, Lieutenant."

Lieutenant Corkin gave me one of those *you're being sassy* looks that Mrs. Kolbacher has perfected.

The only thing that I was grateful for was that Lieutenant Corkin had actually seen me lose the dogfight with the Amalgamated Bauxite Industries helicopter. In my mind, that gave me total credi-bility. Why else would Lieutenant Corkin mobilize THREE ultra-cool Coast Guard Jayhawk heli-copters?

But when we arrived to the exact spot where the mining camp was on the lower half of Mingwa Trail and found NOTHING, ABSOLUTELY NOTH-ING, any trust credits I had with Lieutenant Cor-kin had been spent.

The three helicopters landed in formation. (Chief Petty Officer Eddy was an excellent pilot, and I now felt I was a qualified judge.) I followed Lieutenant Corkin out of the Jayhawk and looked around. The other Coasties did the same. No dump truck, no shovel, no pickups, no tents, no Porta-Johns. Nothing. The only thing I noticed was that the ground was WET, although it hadn't been raining.

"Walker?" Lieutenant Corkin was now using my last name. He had called me "kid" several times, but this was the first time he pulled out "Walker." I did not interpret this as a good omen.

"Where's this *mining camp*? You sure you got the right location?" Lieutenant Corkin crossed his arms over his chest as he spoke—another bad sign.

"They covered their tracks," I said as I tapped my foot on the wet soil.

"*They covered their tracks?* You said they had a three-hundred-and-sixty-ton dump truck!"

I didn't have the courage to tell the lieutenant that the dump truck was by far the smaller of the two earth-moving vehicles. So I said, "They had a road grader. And a water tanker."

"Look, I want to believe you, Walker. But where would someone hide vehicles that big? You said the shovel was eight stories tall."

Lieutenant Corkin had said the thing all the

Coasties were thinking: How could anyone make that much manpower and machinery disappear?

"Look up on Sakemwah Hill. You see all those rocks and debris? They were blasting."

All the Coast Guard guys turned and looked up the hill. It did look thrashed, but you would only know that if you had spent tons of time out here like my friends and I did. When the lieutenant turned back to face me, I could see he was getting impatient. He had just mobilized a squadron of helicopters on the word of a twelve-year-old surfer and possible ultra-light thief and could foresee humiliation in front of his men and disciplinary action by his commanders.

"Where is the mining camp, Walker?"

"Clearly not here. But—" I stopped short. A thought occurred to me. I started striding toward the Jayhawk. "We need to get back in the air!"

"Walker, are you the commander on this mission?"

"No, sir. But I think I know where my friends are."

"You *think* or you *know*?"

"I know that I think I am hoping, sir," I said as I stepped back into the helicopter. Chief Petty Officer Eddy gave me a *you're wasting my valuable time* look.

"Does this copter have thermal imaging?" I asked. Chief Petty Officer Eddy looked at me with contempt. "That's classified."

TITAN GROVE

The important clue was that the earth-moving shovel was *eight stories tall.* The only things in Pine Hollow State Forest that are tall enough to hide a gigantic shovel are the pines of Titan Grove. If Trasker hadn't moved all the men and equipment there, then I was out of ideas. I began to doubt myself and everything I had experienced until I remembered that my six friends, a 243-pound mastiff, an ocicat, and the two boneheads had to be SOMEWHERE out here in the Hollow.

The three Jayhawks were now moving in tight formation at about five hundred feet as I pointed out Titan Grove to Lieutenant Corkin. I knew that he was seconds away from giving the order to return to base.

"Lieutenant Corkin?"

"What?"

"If you had something *like* thermal imaging in the cockpit, couldn't that help you find the mining machines?"

"What do you possibly know about thermal imaging?"

"Next to nothing, sir. But my buddy Wyatt talks about it all the time. He watches a lot of shows about the military on a cable show called *Gear Geeks*." I wish I hadn't included the name of the show. It sounded, well, geeky.

"Well, this isn't cable television, Walker. The sun is still up. Everything is warm. The thermal imaging gear works best at night. Then something like an engine or a person really lights up the grid."

We were now nearing the grove. My friends were counting on me. I had to push Lieutenant Corkin even if it meant him becoming even more annoyed (if that was possible).

"But those mining trucks are so huge that their engines must get really hot. That could show up, right?"

Lieutenant Corkin just stared at me. I knew he had reached a precipice; he was very frustrated. He was the commander of an elite Coast Guard unit, and I was the kid who knocked the radar dish off his motor lifeboat. If I were in his shoes I would have handed me a parachute and told me to jump. Maybe no parachute.

"What are we *doing*, sir?" I could sense a peevish quality in Chief Petty Officer Eddy's voice.

"Turn on the I.R.," Lieutenant Corkin said.

Thermal imaging uses infrared light. Hence the I.R. Wyatt thinks I don't listen to him, but I do. Sometimes.

"But, the ambient heat coefficient—," Petty Officer Eddy started.

"Just do it, Eddy."

I watched as Petty Officer Eddy flicked on a switch. A green video screen came to life. I started to move forward to the cockpit, but Lieutenant Corkin yanked me back in my seat. "Sit. Stay," were the only words he said.

Lieutenant Corkin stood between Eddy and the copilot and examined the screen. From where I was sitting, the I.R. monitor looked like it was filled with blobs of cloudy green mist. The three men in the cockpit said absolutely nothing. Chief Petty Officer Eddy was effortlessly maneuvering the Jayhawk in a grid-search pattern. I saw Lieutenant Corkin lean a little closer to the thermal imaging screen. He pointed at something with his finger.

Now the copilot (I think his nametag read PETTY OFFICER SATER) bent closer to the screen. He looked up at Lieutenant Corkin and said, "What the heck is that?"

"Something big," Lieutenant Corkin said.

"You think it's my friends?" I called to Lieutenant Corkin.

"Shut up, Walker."

"No place to put down," Eddy said.

"Hover." Lieutenant Corkin's voice had completely changed.

I could tell he was in combat mode. Things started happening fast.

"Lower hoists. Deploy on my command."

I heard Chief Petty Officer Eddy relay this information to the other helicopters. Lieutenant Corkin whipped open the door of the helicopter. Even though I had been in the ultra-light, it was startling to be hovering above the huge pine trees with the door open. I could see that a long steel cable was lowering from a winch just above the line of the door. Corkin and his men were reaching for harnesses, which looked a lot like the gear we used to rock climb. I started to reach for one of the harnesses, when Corkin slapped away my hand.

"Don't even think about it, Walker."

"Those are my—" I didn't get the chance to finish my sentence.

"DEPLOY!" Lieutenant Corkin yelled, and he was the first one zipping down the hoist line.

I didn't even wait three seconds. I grabbed a harness and strapped it on. The other Coasties looked confused, wondering if I suffered from some sort of mental deficiency. I didn't give them a chance to stop me—I just clicked on to the hoist cable with this little gadget that a rock climber would have called a body belay, it was basically a little pulley that allowed you to control your descent, and I jumped out of the hatch.

Only one-tenth of a second elapsed before I realized the ENORMOUS difference between ROCK CLIMBING RAPPELLING and COAST GUARD HELICOPTER DEPLOYING: NO ROCKS.

When you rappel down the side of a mountain, you are basically *bouncing* off the rock wall as you descend. You can control your speed in two ways: tension on your line and the amount of push you use with your legs as you bounce off the wall. But when you are coming down a Coast Guard hoist line, you are free falling. Only that little body belay device prevents you from becoming a human meteor.

I've never been to the Coast Guard Academy, but I assume that the Coasties don't let recruits simply jump out of hovering helicopters a hundred and fifty feet above a pine forest. They probably start them at fifteen or twenty feet, maybe off a jungle gym of some sort. Then, after the recruit has built up a level of confidence, they probably raise the height of the deploy in gradual increments. I think that would be the absolute best way to practice a descent on a hoist line, because I would not recommend to anyone what I did.

Here's the problem of rappelling with no rock walls: Your feet bicycle in the air, looking for something to bounce off of. Then this pinwheeling leg action causes you to SPIN as you descend, which feels like you are corkscrewing down the world's steepest waterslide. The SPINNING motion causes the hoist line to sway, which means that as you are dropping down you start moving in big circles, as if the world was one big glass of water and you were a spoon stirring it. This would be bad enough over water or an open field, but HUMUNGOUS old-growth pine trees make it downright dangerous. I found myself whapping against branches, pine needles lashing at my neck, arms, and legs. Even this would have been endurable if I was the only person going down the hoist line. The other Coasties above me had to suffer for my inexperience. I would have been able to survive with a shred of dignity had I not fallen on top of Lieutenant Corkin.

Luckily the lieutenant was built like a middle linebacker, so he merely rolled, grabbed me by the shoulders, and lifted me to my feet.

"I'm giving you fair warning, Walker. I'm going to have your father put in the brig for bringing you into the world. Do I make myself clear?"

"Yes, sir, sir," was the only thing I could think to say.

"Don't patronize me."

I just nodded. I wasn't sure what patronize meant, but I didn't want to do it again.

"Lieutenant Doherty warned me about you. I should have listened."

Uh-oh. Apparently Lieutenant Corkin had done some checking up on me and my friends and somehow had made contact with the Coast Guard officer who had dealt with us down in Willow Key. The last thing I wanted was to get a bad rep with the United States Coast Guard, and yet, I had one.

I looked around. There were eight other Coasties

besides Lieutenant Corkin ready to head into the cathedral of trees that was Titan Grove. The three helicopters were hovering high above us. The lieutenant made a series of hand gestures to his men and they fanned out in some sort of well-rehearsed way. You can tell they all had hours and hours of training. For those of you who don't know much about the Coast Guard, they rock.

Lieutenant Corkin pointed to a spot just behind his right foot and said, "Heel."

Like some sort of border collie, I got into position right behind the lieutenant. I planned on being very obedient from this point forward. I was now part of a platoon.

About three hundred yards into the Titan pines, I heard a small crackle from Lieutenant Corkin's walkie-talkie. He stopped in his tracks. We both peered out from behind a massive pine. There in front of us was the world's largest mining shovel, a gigantic white canvas tent, and a phalanx of trucks and miners. The only three things missing:

1. Mr. Trasker, the foreman
2. The 360-ton dump truck
3. My friends

So much for all the stealth hand signals and fanning-out techniques; the helicopters had been spotted, and we had been expected. A tall, square man in a dark suit was facing us.

MR. MARTIN BRIGGS

"May I help you, gentlemen? I'm Martin Briggs, regional director of Amalgamated Bauxite Industries." Mr. Briggs put out his hand to shake with Lieutenant Corkin as if it was the most natural thing in the world to be in a pine forest confronted by nine Coasties and a twelve-year-old surfer. He almost made it seem like we had interrupted a late-afternoon conference call.

But Lieutenant Corkin didn't shake Martin Briggs's hand. There were only two reasons I could think why Lieutenant Corkin was being rude:

1. I had annoyed Lieutenant Corkin to such a degree that he forgot his manners.
2. Lieutenant Corkin didn't trust Martin Briggs.

I prayed it was the second reason. You have to admit, it was pretty strange that a regional director (whatever that is) dressed in a suit was standing in front of several billion tons of earth-moving equipment concealed in Titan Grove. You wouldn't even find this kind of unexplainable behavior in those ultra-boring French films Jenny Andrews liked to go to.

"I want to speak to your foreman, Trasker," Lieutenant Corkin said.

"No one by that name works for me," Briggs said with perfect ease and conviction.

It seemed to me that Lieutenant Corkin's expression hardened at that moment. He looked like his face was chiseled in granite. Briggs was denying the existence of Trasker? What was happening? Again, two thoughts fired at once:

1. EITHER this confirmed to Lieutenant Corkin that I was insane and had completely fabricated my story OR . . .
2. This confirmed to Lieutenant Corkin that Briggs was lying and trying to cover something up.

Lieutenant Corkin spoke very slowly, as if having to push all emotion out of his voice. "This young man here claims you have his friends in that shovel up there."

"Let's clear that up immediately," Briggs said, and gave a small wave of his hand that looked kind of *rehearsed*.

I knew before the huge shovel lowered to the ground that my friends and the two poser surfers, Hunter and Lance, would not be in it. The shovel lowered to earth with a huge THUD. The ground shook, dust flew, and, as I expected, the shovel was empty.

"Where's the dump truck?" I said to Briggs.

"Shut up, Walker," Lieutenant Corkin said.

"Lieutenant Corkin, can you ask where the three-hundred-and-sixty-ton Caterpillar 797 dump truck is? I'm wondering."

Lieutenant Corkin looked as if he regretted rescuing me from Surf Island Lagoon, but he turned to Briggs and said, "Where is the dump truck?"

"We don't have a three-hundred-and-sixty-ton truck."

Lieutenant Corkin pointed to the huge shovel. "What do you unload that thing into?"

"Various other vehicles that haven't arrived yet," Briggs said.

"You mean haven't arrived here in *Titan Grove*, where you are NOT digging a bauxite mine?"

I wasn't sure, but I think Lieutenant Corkin was now deeply suspicious of Martin Briggs. Things weren't adding up and Lieutenant Corkin was a guy who liked things to add up. You remember how adults sometimes underestimate the intelligence of kids? I think adults who wear suits often underestimate the intelligence of adults who wear uniforms. Mr. Briggs thought Lieutenant Corkin was like some crumb he could brush off the lapel of his jacket. That was a serious mistake.

"What's going on here, Mr. Briggs?"

"Aren't you just a bit out of your jurisdiction, Lieutenant? Shouldn't the Coast Guard be rescuing stranded rowboaters or something?"

Oh boy. Mr. Briggs not only insulted Lieutenant Corkin, he just went off on the United States Coast Guard.

To his credit, Lieutenant Corkin kept his cool. "A felony was committed in my jurisdiction. Assault with a deadly weapon—an Amalgamated Bauxite helicopter tried to chop this young man out of the sky."

Before Mr. Briggs could even open his mouth,

Lieutenant Corkin continued. "Don't even try to deny the existence of the helicopter, because my men and I have it all on digital video. And we also have this." Lt. Corkin threw some Xeroxed papers at Mr. Briggs's feet. "The Amalgamated Bauxite mineral lease that says you, your men, and your equipment shouldn't be here for another five days."

So Lieutenant Corkin *had* checked out my story before we flew out here. He had just been giving me a hard time, maybe for lopping off his radar tower.

Martin Briggs didn't even bother picking up the papers.

"It doesn't matter what it says on that lease," Mr. Briggs said.

"I think it does," Lieutenant Corkin said. "And I think the Department of the Interior will think so as well."

"You don't have the juice, Lieutenant. Whether you like it or not, Sakemwah Hill will be blasted away by tomorrow. That's how things in the *real world* work."

"Where are those kids?" Lieutenant Corkin didn't allow himself to get caught up in any global arguments.

"I tell you what, Lieutenant. You let us finish our

work on that hill, and we'll help you find whom-
ever you're looking for. Make sure they are safe and
sound."

Okay, there it was. Mr. Briggs wanted to make
sure NO ONE GOT IN HIS WAY blowing up
Sakemwah Hill. He must have FIGURED OUT
that the discovery of the lost Indian village would
stop the mine project indefinitely. Sakemwah Hill
had gone from being a local curiosity to a site of
historic importance like the Alamo. Mr. Briggs was
basically HOLDING MY FRIENDS HOSTAGE,
using them as a bargaining chip so that Amalgamated Bauxite Industries could have their mine.
Maybe Hunter was right; maybe big *does* win.

And then I heard Howie bark.

I didn't hesitate for a millisecond—I ran in the
direction of the sound.

"WALKER!" Lieutenant Corkin yelled.

"GRAB HIM!" Mr. Briggs yelled.

That's when I knew I was headed in the right
direction. I sprinted right toward the huge, white
canvas tent. Maybe my friends and Howie were
being held there. Miners were diving, trying to
tackle me to prevent me from getting to the tent. I
told you earlier, I'm pretty fast (maybe not as fast as

Bettina), and I zigzagged through the miners like a running back weaving his way through the defense. I was about forty yards from the tent when I heard a GIANT ENGINE ROAR TO LIFE.

The next thing I knew the tent (which seemed to be the size of a football field) WAS RIPPED OUT OF THE GROUND, and the Caterpillar 797 emerged from a RAMP that had been dug SIXTY FEET into the ground. It looked like a monstrous tarantula lunging out of its spider hole. For an instant I could see Mr. Trasker behind the wheel, but I had to DIVE OUT OF THE WAY to avoid being steamrolled by the dump truck's thirteen-feet-high tires.

In the confusion I heard more barking. It was coming from inside the dump bed. I could now also hear my friends yelling. But there was nothing I could do to stop the world's largest dump truck. Even the Coasties couldn't take the risk of getting in front of the three-story-high vehicle. They all jumped out of the way, except for Lieutenant Corkin, who pushed a miner away from an Amalgamated Bauxite pickup truck and climbed in. Before he was even able to turn the key, I leaped into the passenger seat. Lieutenant Corkin glared at me but didn't have time to do anything but put the pickup in gear and zoom after the monster dump truck. Trasker was going to try and outrun the United States Coast Guard.

CHASING A CATERPILLAR

You would think that the Caterpillar 797 would be slow. But it's not. It has an engine that has enough horsepower to run a small city. It is supposed to lug up to 360 tons of ore and now it was only carrying Wyatt, Bettina, Shelby, Ty, Din, Nar, Hunter, Lance, Howie, and Ki. Even with Howie in the mix, all of them together didn't weigh more than a thousand pounds. That means the Caterpillar had buckets of power for the task at hand, which was, at this moment, plowing along Mingwa Trail at top speed.

It is hard to describe how much dirt, pine needles, and full-size rocks the thirteen-foot Caterpillar tires kick up when barreling along a dirt trail. Lieutenant Corkin and I, trailing behind in the ABI pickup, were being pelted with debris. It was hard to see through the backwash of dirt and the flickering late-afternoon light shafting through the pines. But we did see ONE END OF A STATIC LINE FALL FROM THE REAR OF THE TRUCK BED.

Lieutenant Corkin pounded the steering wheel with one of his fists. "You've got to be kidding me! Are all your friends as idiotic as you are?"

"I'm afraid so, sir." I decided I had to tell the truth; it could save my friends.

Lieutenant Corkin grabbed his walkie-talkie and yelled into it, "Chief Eddy! You tracking that huge dump truck?"

"Affirmative, sir. There's a bunch of kids and a really big dog inside of it."

"Tell me something I don't know, Chief!" Lieutenant Corkin slammed his fist on the steering wheel again.

Chief Petty Officer Eddy took his commander seriously. "I think they are trying to climb out of the thing."

"Copy that. Just stay with us—this thing could get sloppy."

"Copy."

Wyatt would have enjoyed all of this cool Coast Guard walkie-speak—that is, if he hadn't been trapped in the world's largest dump truck rocketing along Mingwa Trail.

"Oh, no," Lieutenant Corkin said when he saw Ty make it to the rear edge of the dump bed. He was planning to belay down the static rope, which was flapping behind the dump truck. Ty looked surprised when he saw the ABI pickup trailing behind the Caterpillar. I stuck my head out of the passenger window and started waving. Ty pumped his fist in the air; he was happy to see a friendly face.

"HOLD ON, WALKER!" Lieutenant Corkin yelled as he floored the pickup. We were directly behind the huge dump truck, which was a good thing in one respect: Our pickup was so small and the Caterpillar so amazingly WIDE that we must have been invisible to Mr. Trasker up in the cab. In another respect, we were right in the vortex of dust and debris kicked up by the huge wheels. As we neared the rear of the truck, we were in a hurricane of pine needles and pebbles.

I understood what Lieutenant Corkin was trying to do. The dump bed was so gigantic; it OVER-HUNG the rear wheels like a shelf. It would be possible to DRIVE UNDERNEATH the overhang and have Ty rappel into our pickup truck's tiny bed. Of course if the dump truck stopped, we would crash into the world's largest commercially produced transaxle and crumple up like aluminum foil.

But there was no time to think, only to act. Ty was already zipping down the rope and Lieutenant Corkin squeezed the pickup into position. In two seconds Ty had hopped into the pickup bed.

He yelled to me through the sliding rear window, "Where been you?"

"Long story," I called back.

Ty held the end of the rope so Bettina could zip down into the pickup. I saw Ki's little nose poking out of her day pack. We heard the gears of the dump truck grinding. Immediately Lieutenant Corkin slowed our pickup so we could drop back and not crash into the underbelly of the Caterpillar. We saw Hunter poised on the lip of the dump bed. He was wondering whether or not to descend.

The Caterpillar was now picking up speed again, heading up Mingwa Trail toward the original site of the mining camp. Lieutenant Corkin accelerated and got underneath the dump truck in time for Hunter, Lance, Shelby, and Wyatt to rappel down the static line.

Wyatt leaned close to the sliding rear window of the pickup and said, "Big problem."

Wyatt could have said:

1. "Thanks for saving our lives."
2. "It is awesome you brought the Coast Guard with you."
3. "I'm happy to be alive."

But Wyatt said none of those things because he is, at the end of the day, Wyatt Kolbacher.

Lieutenant Corkin was very tensed out about the potential of crashing into the Caterpillar, so he said, "HOW MANY OTHER KIDS ARE UP THERE?"

Wyatt said, "That's the big problem. Nar won't come down without Howie, and Din won't come down without Nar."

"Please don't tell me Howie is the dog. Please don't tell me that!" Lieutenant Corkin said. "We'll worry about the dog LATER!"

"Nar doesn't roll that way," Wyatt said.

Lieutenant Corkin applied the breaks and let the pickup drift back behind the behemoth dump truck. I didn't know the lieutenant very well, but I think he was now regretting his choice to spend his life in public service. Or maybe he was worried about all of our safety. Probably a little bit of both. He grabbed his walkie-talkie.

"Chief Eddy! Lower the rescue basket, NOW!"

"Copy that, sir!" We then heard Chief Petty Officer Eddy yell to his copilot, "Sater, send down the big basket! That dog is HUGE!"

I looked out the passenger window to see the rescue basket being lowered from the Jayhawk. The basket kind of looked like a big snowshoe dangling beneath the helicopter.

The Caterpillar rounded a bend in the trail. Since we had dropped a safe distance behind the massive vehicle, Trasker caught sight of us in his rearview mirror. That's when the really bad stuff started to happen.

Trasker decided to LIFT THE DUMP BED and DUMP out his "load," which was Din, Nar, and Howie. My guess is that Mr. Trasker had switched plans from *kidnap the witnesses* to *run and hide*. The basket had just lowered into the truck bed. Din and Nar were furiously strapping on Howie, who, even while the truck bed was slowly rising and a helicopter hovered overhead, kept his same calm, unworried demeanor.

Not so for Din and Nar. They were frantically trying to make sure Howie was secure before they could think about saving themselves. As the dump bed was rising, they were SLIDING toward the lip. They had about two seconds before they would be thrown off the back of the truck (which was still HAULING full speed along the trail).

Din and Nar did the only thing they could at the moment: They grabbed onto the hoist rope, putting their legs on either side of Howie. This violated about six billion safety rules of the Coast Guard, but the Coasties in the copter alertly LIFTED the RESCUE BASKET, and Din, Nar, and Howie soared above the level of the open dump bed—which now towered FIVE STORIES above the trail—and flew up into the sky. The uneven weight distribution caused them to begin to spin. I couldn't help thinking that they looked like some type of bad circus act called "Two Small Guys and a Big Dog." I didn't share this amusing thought with Lieutenant Corkin as he seemed to be focusing all his energies on avoiding the apocalypse.

THE APOCALYPSE

Lieutenant Corkin jammed on the brakes and came to a skidding stop. We were very lucky that all my friends in the ABI pickup were not thrown to the road, but that would have been preferable to what happened to Mr. Trasker.

I don't know anything about driving a huge construction vehicle, but I can guess that the operator of the Caterpillar 797 is not supposed to LIFT THE DUMP BED while DRIVING AT FULL SPEED. The reason for this is obvious: As the bed rises so high into the air, the truck becomes more likely to TIP—especially if the open truck bed HITS SOME MASSIVE PINE TREE BRANCHES.

I don't want you to think that the pine branches knocked over the truck; that happened later. What the pine branches did is cause the truck to ALMOST TIP OVER. Mr. Trasker, perhaps realizing his mistake in raising the dump bed, tried to keep control of the vehicle but couldn't manage. The Caterpillar 797 SMASHED into a huge boulder on the side of Sakemwah Hill, not that far from the vent we had all used to escape from the pottery room in the lost village. The dump truck stalled. We could hear Mr. Trasker trying to get the huge engine back in gear. Maybe Mr. Trasker was looking down at his gauges and dials, maybe he was trying to yank the gear shift, but I don't think he could have done anything even if he'd had warning.

A Caterpillar 797 is so huge that under normal circumstances it could absorb a high-speed collision with a massive boulder. But what the humungous truck could not survive was a confrontation with an underground river.

Somehow the Caterpillar 797 (maybe in combination with the dynamiting) had punctured a hole in the rock wall that contained the underground river running through the Sakemwah village. Remember that whole thing about water being trapped in a confined space and then being able to run free? Well this river had been forced underground hundreds of years ago and was really ready to see the sunlight again.

I've never been to New York City but I've seen a lot of pictures of the Empire State Building. Imagine a fireman being as tall as that building. Then picture the enormous size of the fire hose the skyscraper-tall fireman would have in his hands. Then think of the size of the FURIOUS TORRENT of water that would GUSH out of that fire hose. Now see that deluge of water hitting a Caterpillar 797 (with its dump bed raised) on the *broadside* and TIPPING IT OVER like a child flicks over a domino. Then you can understand why the newly released river enveloped the 360-ton truck and send it hurtling down Sakemwah Hill in a cascade of white water.

We all watched Mr. Trasker climb out the window of the huge dump truck. He now looked like a man atop the world's largest and heaviest raft, being carried down a level five rapids. It was as if Mingwa, the river chief, was taking revenge on all those who had betrayed him and the Sakemwah. The Outriders might have stumbled on the lost village, but the Titan pines, the subterranean river, and the spirit of Mingwa were ultimately the forces that defeated Amalgamated Bauxite Industries. But I'm getting ahead of myself. There's a bunch of stuff you have to know first.

CHAPTER TEN: SURVEYING

Chief Petty Officer Eddy was hovering the Jayhawk directly overhead. Howie, still strapped to the rescue basket, descended from the heavens with Din and Nar standing at his side. The moment the sled touched the earth, we all ran out of the pickup and helped release the mastiff. Everyone was making a big fuss over Howie, giving him pats and kisses. Even Ki climbed out of Bettina's day pack and took up residence on Howie's back. Howie took it all in stride as he normally does, with droopy eyes and a slowly wagging tail.

Din's first words were: "That was way cool."

Nar said, "Howie liked it."

Then Hunter said, "How can you tell?"

Nar narrowed his eyes, ready to pounce on Hunter.

"He was just bustin' chops, brah!" Lance said to Nar.

Lieutenant Corkin's walkie-talkie crackled. He hadn't taken his eyes off Mr. Trasker. The mining foreman was completely stranded on top of his enormous Caterpillar 797.

I heard Chief Petty Officer Eddy say, "Lieutenant?"

"Go," was all Lieutenant Corkin said.

"You want us to save that guy on the truck?"

"No," Lieutenant Corkin said. Then after a long wait he said, "But we have to."

"Why's that, sir?"

"Because we are the United States Coast Guard."

"Roger that," Chief Petty Officer Eddy said as he expertly maneuvered his helicopter over Mr. Trasker.

I thought it was kind of cool that we were about to witness the first rescue on a new river. But then it occurred to me that this river had always been here—it was Sternmetz and his men that had changed its course and forced it underground. The powerful river was now widening the gaping hole in Sakemwah Hill. When the sun was at the right angle, it was possible to get a glimpse into the lost Indian village. It gave me hope that sometime soon things would return to the way they were supposed to be. I just hoped that there wouldn't be another Sternmetz or Amalgamated Bauxite to ruin things.

We all watched as Mr. Trasker was lifted off the world's largest dump truck. Chief Petty Officer Eddy then swung the Jayhawk over to a clearing and gently lowered Mr. Trasker toward the ground, where five Coasties were waiting to arrest him. I guess that's why Mr. Trasker jumped off the rescue basket when it was still five feet in the air and bolted into the forest.

I think this bold maneuver caught the Coasties completely by surprise. I guess they underestimated how desperate and ruthless the foreman was. But then the strangest thing happened: Mr. Trasker came running BACK OUT OF THE WOODS. He seemed to be running TWICE AS FAST as when he ran in! Two of the Coasties grabbed him. Mr. Trasker put up quite a struggle but the handcuffs quieted him down.

That's when we saw the bear.

A big black bear (was it the same one we saw earlier? I have no idea; I don't know much about bears) burst out of the trees and stopped at the edge of the clearing. It stood on its hind legs and kind of ROARED (maybe it was a BELLOW) and bared its teeth. Even the ultra-brave Coasties reacted as I had: They froze.

The bear seemed to be looking directly at Mr. Trasker. I know some people think animals aren't capable of great intelligence or emotions. But Mr. Mora, who knows more about living things than just about anyone, once said, "People who think animals don't have emotions are people who don't know animals." Now I'm not sure that this bear understood that Mr. Trasker was a human who planned to destroy Pine Hollow, but I was sure that this bear did not want Mr. Trasker in its forest.

As quickly as the bear appeared, it turned and retreated into the Hollow.

Lieutenant Corkin was now out of the pickup truck. "Did that just happen?" he said.

Before I could reply, I noticed Lance and Hunter had started off-loading arrowheads, pottery shards, and carved stones pipes from their cargo pants' pockets and were putting the contraband on the ground.

"We want to turn this stuff in, Mr. Coast Guard Dude," Lance said to Lieutenant Corkin.

Hunter was looking down at all the antiquities. "We thought . . . this would, uh . . . prove to everyone we found that village . . . you know, like archeology-ists or something . . ."

"We don't want to mess with this stuff," Lance said as he looked toward Mr. Trasker in handcuffs. "It's got bad mojo."

"If you all don't mind, we're gonna boogie and fly away home," Hunter said, about to march up the Trail toward Eagle tower. "It's been a long one."

Lieutenant Corkin looked at me.

"Hey, Hunter . . . there's kind of a problem with one of the ultra-lights."

"Micro-lights," Wyatt corrected me.

"Yeah? What kind of problem?" Hunter said.

"I have some bad news."

"Not from you, brah! You saved our lives," Lance said.

"One of your planes, the blue one, is sort of at the bottom of Surf Island Lagoon."

Hunter was silent for a moment. "Dude, you're joking right?"

"Nope. I used it to go get help."

"You a pilot?"

"Not a good one."

I could see Hunter was upset about the plane. He looked like a guy who was going to have to explain something HUGE to his parents. But he didn't complain. He understood I had no other option.

Wyatt looked at Hunter and said, "My dad has a marine salvage yard. We'll dredge it up."

Lance actually put his arm on my shoulder. "Stuff happens, right, BK?"

"BK?" I said.

"Big kahuna, brah!"

In his push to be surfer cool, Lance was perhaps the uncoolest person I'd ever met. But at least he and Hunter recognized that my friends and I had pulled them out of some tight spots, so I didn't dislike them as much as I did at the beginning of the day.

I realized the sun was beginning to set. Lieutenant Corkin offered to ferry us back to Surf Island.

"Would you mind dropping us at Shady Cove? We've got our canoes stashed there," I said.

"It's getting late; won't your parents be worried?"

"Nope, we were supposed to do an overnight."

"Why don't you get the canoes tomorrow?" Lieutenant Corkin said.

"It's better if we do it tonight," Shelby said.

"Because the canoes don't belong to you?" Lieutenant Corkin put his hands on his hips.

"No comment," Bettina said.

THE DAY GETS LONGER

By sundown Shelby, Wyatt, Bettina, Ty, Din, Nar, Howie, Ki, and I were paddling across Surf Island Lagoon in the Old Town Trippers. All was peaceful out on the water; the only sounds were the splashes our paddles made as they dipped into the water. The lagoon was like a dark mirror reflecting a full moon. Each of us was exhausted, but it had been a day to top all days. But I would discover it was far from over.

Bettina broke the long silence. "After we return the canoes, maybe we should all go to my house."

Shelby said, "Absolutely."

Obviously Bettina wanted us to get a chance to say good-bye to Mr. Conroy and wish him luck. Also she probably needed some company.

After we returned the Old Towns to the Bluffs Yachting and Beach Club (yes, we hosed them down and cleaned them perfectly, don't worry), we walked over to Bettina's house. Bettina was cradling Ki in her arms. The ocicat was purring steadily.

Bettina and her family live on the second floor of an old house. The first floor is home to the Conroy family business, the Cut Hut. Even though it was late and the Cut Hut should have been closed up for the night, all the lights were on at the barber shop/ salon.

Through the rectangular plate glass window that advertised PERMS—$29.00, BOYS' HAIRCUTS— $9.00, we could see Mrs. Conroy and Viveca hugging Mr. Conroy, who was dressed in his army fatigues. Bettina handed Ki to Shelby and raced up the front stairs of the Cut Hut and yanked open the door.

The rest of us just hung out on the porch, but we could hear everything that was going on. Mr. Conroy opened his arms and lifted Bettina into a hug.

"Dad, what's going on?" Bettina said.

"Daddy's orders got changed. He's leaving tonight," Mrs. Conroy said. "We had no way to reach you out there in Pine Hollow."

"I thought I wasn't going to get a chance to say good-bye," Mr. Conroy said. "I'm so glad you got back early."

Bettina had tears in her eyes. "So am I." She hugged her dad really tightly.

"Dad, tell them you cut hair. The army needs barbers, don't they?" Viveca said.

"I'll let the army know." Mr. Conroy was smiling, but there didn't seem much behind it.

The rest of us didn't know what to do. We felt like we were intruding, but we didn't just want to disappear in case Bettina needed us. Mrs. Conroy spotted us on the porch and waved us inside. It got really crowded inside the Cut Hut since Howie felt he had to be in there as well. Viveca took Ki from Shelby and nuzzled the cat. It looked like it was something she needed to do.

Mr. Conroy has dark skin and keeps his hair trimmed really close to his head. He has kind of bushy eyebrows that dance around a lot when he cracks jokes as he gives you a haircut. But his eyebrows weren't moving at all when he said, "I'm glad you're all here. I've got to go do this thing for a while, and Mrs. Conroy, Viveca, and Bettina might need some extra help. And that's what families do; help each other out, right?"

"Don't worry, we're here," was all I could think to say.

"Please to excuse me," Ty said. He then reached into his pocket and pulled something out. When he opened his hand we all saw he was holding a strange foreign coin (maybe from Ty's country). It had a number five on one side, and a horse dancing over some stars on the other. He held it out for Mr. Conroy.

"Is for luck," Ty said.

"I can't accept this, Ty. It's yours," Mr. Conroy said.

"I no need," Ty motioned to all of us. "I am luck having."

Bettina took the coin from Ty and put it in her father's front uniform pocket, right next to his heart. Mr. Conroy patted the pocket.

"And now I am luck having," he said.

None of us said a word. I felt something strange happening to the corners of my eyes. (Maybe dust from flying the ultra-light without goggles?)

My dad opened the front door and said, "What

happened to the overnight? You kids see a bear or something?"

In tough times, my dad likes to try to "lighten the mood." Sometimes this technique works, sometimes it doesn't. This time I think it worked pretty well, because Shelby said, "As a matter of fact, we did see a bear. Twice."

"Did you play dead? I hear that's what you have to do."

A few of us laughed and my father had done his job.

My guess was that Dad had come by to take Mr. Conroy to the bus station in Ellistown. He handed Mr. Conroy two cigars. "These cost three bucks a piece, so don't smoke them all at once."

Mr. Conroy tucked them into his knapsack and said, "I'm going to save them for when I get back."

"Good, then I'll smoke one," Dad said, and picked up Mr. Conroy's knapsack. Then my dad looked at me. "I got a message on the machine from a Lieutenant Corkin. Anything I should know?"

"I'll tell you all about it later." I didn't think the Conroys needed any additional burdens.

"Am I going to be happy when I hear the story?" my dad asked.

"Probably not," I said.

"Everyone is okay, though?" Mrs. Conroy said.

"Absolutely," Shelby said with her most winning smile.

My dad took the knapsack down the front steps and we all followed. We let Bettina, Viveca, and Mrs. Conroy say their last good-byes, and then my father drove Mr. Conroy off to Ellistown.

As I watched the car recede down Surf Island Boulevard, I thought about how my dad and Mr. Conroy grew up together and had each other as best friends. Both of them worked really hard, so we Outriders could go off into Pine Hollow and discover lost villages. Now Mr. Conroy was going off to a really scary situation, all because he was trying to get good insurance for his family. And now Mrs. Conroy would have to run the Cut Hut on her own. I decided that I was going to take my time growing up; being an adult doesn't look so easy when you see it up close.

Mrs. Conroy and Viveca took Ki upstairs to give her a bowl of cream. Without anyone saying a word, Ki had been adopted by the Conroys. I think Ki needed a family and the Conroys needed Ki.

The rest of us were just hanging out on the curb,

when out of nowhere, Bettina yelled, "COWA-BUNGA, DUDE!"

I don't know why she thought to say it, but we all started laughing so hard tears came to our eyes. You know that kind of laughing where once you start, you can't stop? That was what was happening. It was hard to explain, but it felt really good, even if it was tough to catch my breath. I actually had to sit down, I was laughing so hard. That's when a black Rolls Royce limousine glided to a stop in front of the Cut Hut.

No one in the Flats has a Rolls Royce limousine (duh) and only one person in the Bluffs owns one: Mr. Chapman Thorpe.

Here's the thing about Mr. Thorpe: He knows everything. He's not like a sorcerer or wizard or anything—he is just insanely well-connected. I was 100 percent certain that Mr. Thorpe:

1. Knew every detail of our midnight ride with Galloway
2. Had been briefed by the Coast Guard about the events in the Hollow
3. Was here for a specific reason

The darkly tinted rear window lowered and Mr. Thorpe's face appeared.

"Hello, Mr. Thorpe," I said as I stood up and walked toward the limo.

"Chappy. Hello, Cam."

Mr. Thorpe always wanted me to call him by his nickname but it simply was never going to happen.

Mr. Thorpe didn't get out of the limousine. Something was wrong with his legs and he had to walk with these complicated-looking aluminum crutches. He had a long nose and intense blue eyes. I wasn't sure I could trust Mr. Thorpe, but I wasn't completely suspicious of him either. All I knew for certain was that whenever I was around him I had to stay very alert.

"You all must be famished after your adventure today."

See? This was Mr. Thorpe's way of letting us all know that he had heard about what went down in Pine Hollow. Also he used words like "famished," which I believe was another technique to throw us off balance. I had no way of competing with Mr. Thorpe on the mind-game playing field, but I always gave it my best shot.

"We were just about to call you," I said.

"Is that so?" Mr. Thorpe has this weird smile that shows a bunch of teeth and looks more like a frown.

"You will never guess what we found at Eagle Tower," I said, trying to put a glint of mystery in my voice.

"You've read my mind. I wanted to speak to all of you about Eagle Tower."

I looked over at my friends. I think they felt sorry for me. There was no way on earth I was going to stay ahead of Mr. Thorpe.

"Giorgio has made a beautiful dinner; I'd like to invite you all to be my guests at Falcon's Lair. It sounds like we have a lot to discuss."

I didn't even have to check with anyone. We all knew we were going. We had made too many cool discoveries, and Mr. Thorpe was the only person on earth who had enough information to under-stand it all.

"Mr. Thorpe, I'd love to go, but . . ." Bettina had trouble finishing her sentence.

"Please give my best to your family, Bettina." Mr. Thorpe was being kind and letting us know that he was aware Mr. Conroy had been deployed.

That's why you always had to be on alert around "Chappy." Bettina gave Shelby a hug (something she didn't normally do) and went up the stairs to her house. Ty sat down on the Cut Hut steps as if he planned to stay there for the rest of his life. We didn't even bother asking him to join us.

After it was resolved that the limousine had enough room to include Howie, the rest of us piled into the Rolls Royce and were whisked away to Falcon's Lair.

ANOTHER SECRET REVEALED

I'm not sure if Giorgio cooks the food himself or if there are other people who do that for Mr. Thorpe, but everything we've eaten at Falcon's Lair has been really awesome. Sometimes I think about a pizza I had there and remember it as number one on the all-time pizza list (which is a really high compliment). Over dinner we told Mr. Thorpe everything about the lost Sakemwah village, the cave paintings, and the numerous crossings of the underground river. But I was saving my best info for later.

After dinner Mr. Thorpe had Shelby, Wyatt, Din, Nar, and me come into the solarium where his office was. It took Mr. Thorpe a long time to get there with his crutches.

"I want to show you all something," Mr. Thorpe said as he took a seat at his massive desk and pulled out a plastic-laminated piece of a map.

We had all seen this partial map before. It was a map from the olden days that Mr. Thorpe had found in El Trueno's ship's log. The map depicted half of the football of Surf Island.

"I contracted a cartographer to complete the map using current satellite photographs." Mr. Thorpe then unrolled a brand-new map that incorporated the section of old map.

Then Mr. Thorpe picked up El Trueno's sword. It's a long story, but we had recovered the sword while diving the wreck of *L'Esperanza* down in Willow Key (see my last blog). The only important thing to know is the sword has three DIAMOND-SHAPED HOLES evenly spaced on the blade. The letters *ORO* (which means "gold" in Spanish) appear over the diamond holes, one letter over each hole. On El Trueno's partial map, there is ONE diamond shape that perfectly matches the holes on the sword. We all had a feeling that the missing section of map had two other diamond shapes and would somehow, someway, be used in conjunction with the sword to point out a clue to the treasure's location.

"Take a look at what happens when I lay the sword on the map facing *north*." Mr. Thorpe placed the sword on top of the map and lined up the diamond hole nearest the hilt with the one existing diamond from the olden-day map. We all gasped.

When lined up this way, the tip of the sword pointed directly to EAGLE TOWER!

"Oh. My. God," Shelby said. "Cam, tell him what we found."

Instead of talking, I walked over to a mahogany box that was on a long side table. I opened the box and pulled out the Golden Sextant. I tilted the sextant upward so that the bottom of it was revealed to Mr. Thorpe. He had a clear view of the engraving of an eagle, wings outstretched, the fiery orb of the sun balanced between the tips.

"We found this," I said.

BACK TO THE HOLLOW

Mr. Thorpe has a seaplane, a PBY Catalina to be exact. We're pretty sure he also has a jet. But until very early the next morning we had no idea that he had a Sikorsky S92 Helibus. I think the Sikorsky helicopter people did a good job naming it because the S92 looks as if someone took a huge helicopter rotor and stuck it on top of a city bus. It had no problem taking Mr. Thorpe, Giorgio, Shelby, Bettina, Wyatt, Ty, Din, Nar, Howie, and me back to Eagle Tower.

I could tell Bettina was thinking about her dad. But being on an expedition with her family of friends was probably about the best thing she could do.

As for me, this was my third helicopter trip in the past twenty-four hours. Life doesn't get much better than that.

My thoughts were interrupted by Mr. Thorpe when he said, "What shall we do about the marina?"

You would think it was an odd question coming out of the blue like that, but Mr. Thorpe rolled that way.

"What about it?" Wyatt said. Surf Island Salvage was on one side of the marina, so Wyatt had a vested interest.

"We need to rename it. I do not think any landmark should glorify the memory of Commodore Sternmetz."

"But do you think the town is just going to let

the name be changed? How's that going to work?" Shelby said.

"Submit a list of new names to me no later than next Friday," Mr. Thorpe said, and then didn't say anything more.

We landed on the Table, almost in the exact spot where the two ultra-lights had been parked the day before.

The Sikorsky S92 also had a huge cargo area where Mr. Thorpe had stowed something called a scissor lift. This was a rectangular platform that could raise and lower using hydraulics. The reason Mr. Thorpe needed to bring it along was that there was no way on earth he would be able to climb Eagle Tower with his bad legs. Our plan was to take the Golden Sextant up to the spot we had found the eagle carved into the stone. We would see if the sextant fit into the slot. Then we would look through it.

Fifteen minutes after we landed, the scissor lift was in place at the base of the tower. The lift wasn't big enough to hold all of us. I suggested that Ty go up with Mr. Thorpe because he had discovered the eagle. It killed me that I wouldn't be along for the first ride up, but fair was fair.

Ty shook his head. He pointed at me. He wasn't very comfortable around Mr. Thorpe (none of us were) and he viewed me as the person with the "closest" relationship with the guy.

"If Cam's going, I'm going," Shelby said. As I told you, she hates to be left out of any adventure.

So it was settled. Shelby and I hopped onto the platform and Giorgio helped Mr. Thorpe lift first one twisted leg up and then the other. As we rose slowly alongside the tower, we were able to look down on the hole that Howie had dug into a lost world. The hole was now impassable.

"I hope you're both aware you saved Pine Hollow," Mr. Thorpe said.

"What?" was all I could think to say.

"Amalgamated Bauxite Industries no longer has a mineral lease here or anywhere else in the United States."

"Did you do that, Mr. Thorpe?" I had to know.

"Their greed did that," he said.

"But could someone else come here and dig a mine?" Shelby said.

"Not after you found the lost Sakemwah village. All this land will now come under the protection of the Bureau of Indian Affairs. No one will touch Pine Hollow ever again."

I felt intensely good. It was as if big didn't win all the time. Shelby was smiling. The sun was just coming up, and in the dawn light her face looked all glowing and happy.

"Mr. Thorpe, it's seven in the morning. All this happened *yesterday*. How did you find all this out?"

Mr. Thorpe just smiled his frown-smile and let Shelby and me wonder.

When we reached the level of the eagle carved into the stone, the first thing we did was take the Golden Sextant out of the mahogany box. The etching of the eagle at the base of the sextant was an exact match to the one in the stone. Now for the moment of truth. Mr. Thorpe gave me the sextant and I carefully lined up the one-inch golden stem with the hole carved into the stone. I lowered the sextant and—IT WAS A PERFECT FIT!

"We are so going to find the treasure!" Shelby said.

I had my climbing harness on and quickly clipped on a carabiner and let myself down into the opening of the tower. I was now going to look through the

Golden Sextant in the exact spot where the pirate El Trueno looked through it hundreds of years before. I lowered my eye to the small telescope and prepared to solve a long-concealed mystery. I looked through the eyepiece and I saw—the sky.

"CAM, WHAT DO YOU SEE?" Shelby was having trouble controlling her volume; I was only three feet away from her.

"Nothing. The sky."

"What's this?" Mr. Thorpe pointed to a line etched into the bricks that framed the opening. It was easy to see why we had missed it; it was just an angled line that looked like part of the construction of the doorway.

"Align the sextant at that angle," Mr. Thorpe seemed slightly excited as well. He didn't get away from Falcon's Lair that often. Even he was having fun. It was easier for Shelby to adjust the sextant from where she was sitting, and now I lowered my eyes to look again.

What I saw was so cool, it took my breath away.

"WHAT DO YOU SEE?" Shelby was frustrated that I hadn't spoken.

"A diamond," I said.

"WHAT *DIAMOND*?" Shelby was going out of

her mind. I was going to have to let her take a turn.

The sextant was aimed at Surf Island. More accurately, it was aimed at a one-mile-wide section of the Bluffs just below Falcon's Lair. Even more amazing was the fact that the natural rock formations and geography of the one-mile-wide area was in the exact shape of a DIAMOND.

Shelby almost pushed me down into Eagle Tower, she was so eager to get behind the telescope. I explained in detail what I had seen to Mr. Thorpe.

As soon as Shelby looked through the eyepiece she said, "Oh. My. God. We found it!"

"I think we have a *clue*. That is a pretty big area you describe," Mr. Thorpe said.

"But it's another clue! We're solving the puzzle!" Shelby was really caught up in the whole thing.

"I have to believe we are getting closer," Mr. Thorpe said.

"We're going to search that area of the Bluffs, right?" Shelby wanted to go there right *now*, you could tell.

Mr. Thorpe's blue eyes seemed lit up from inside. He might have been ultra-old and his legs might not have worked that well, but he had the same curiosity we did.

Shelby felt compelled to ask the question again, "We're going to search for the treasure, right?"

We were going to do much more than that. But I'll tell you about it in my next blog, *Expedition to Surf Island*. It's too cool a story to rush into.

Are you ready for the final expedition?

FROM THE BLOG OF CAM WALKER

When I'm out in the water on a surfboard, I have to be prepared for surprises. The wind could shift, there could be a sudden riptide, or I might even spot the fin of a shark. So I'm not bragging or anything, but surprises have never rattled me that much.

Except when my mother returned to Surf Island.

And she brought a whole suitcase full of surprises with her:

1. A crucial clue to the secret location of the missing treasure
2. A strange connection to the richest, most powerful guy in our town
3. A bunch of really bad dudes who were coming after her to collect on a debt

I could roll with most of it, but there was one thing that did rattle me— trying to figure out if my mom intended to stay or leave.

But I don't want to spoil any of the surprises. . . .

BE ON THE LOOKOUT FOR

EXPEDITION TO SURF ISLAND